# GUILD WITHOUT A NAME

## A Superhero Epic

## JAIME MERA

# Dedication

I dedicate this book to my friend Lee A. Forrest, and beloved children. Everyone has wonderful and inspiring dreams to become someone or achieve extraordinary goals, but it is in the written world of science fiction that some almost impossible dreams full of adventures can be experienced through the eyes of a superhero. A superhero with strengths and faults like all of us, faults that people may say are evil or selfish, but a hero is not labeled for just the actions on the outside but more what is on the inside, with a hero's heart of courage and love.

Guild Without a Name, A Superhero Epic

# Preface

T he world mourned the death of the greatest superhero of his time, Nuetronium. He was leader of the first superhero group in the world during a time of the Cold War when futures were uncertain. But fate would have it that unique humans and superhumans formed a pack to continue the fight for justice and the pursuit of happiness. The second superhero group was called Energy, Fire and Light; a four member group with sheer power to change the world; however, they had limitations, not in power, but simply that destiny would not put them in the right place at the right time. What they couldn't do, the most recent and most diverse group of heroes could. The Eternal Champions was that superhero group which was uniquely balanced by power, leadership, family unity, resources, and allies. They made their mark on society more than once, and showed the world that it was not power alone that superhumans possessed, but more importantly - compassion for your fellow person. What made superhero groups a driving force against crime, was that they were respected or feared by all. Super villains and organizations were in constant battle with the forces of good and within their own ranks.

The era of super villain groups and uniquely formed alliances would come about, because of superheroes and due to influences outside of Earth. Alien technology and agendas placed Earth in the middle of galactic war. Almost all humans and superhumans were ignorant to the catastrophic future to come, but there was one supreme superhuman that changed the outcome of the human race. His decisions started a chain reaction which would place people together and their unity and actions would forge a powerful weapon against the dark war to come.

Cardigan International, a private foundation, established in the late 1980s broke all the rules and attempted to create the ultimate weapon. The experiments which they gave birth to would come back to haunt them as they fight amongst themselves and kill all who oppose them. A young group of superhumans who escaped the foundation find themselves revisiting the past in exchange for a better future at all costs.

A thief guild comprised of an unlikely friendship of superhumans with a dark past and equally questionable present would emerge to place no allegiance to anyone except themselves. Their actions would shift military power into the wrong hands, and threaten the stability of many countries. This is their stories as the two groups confound the basic premise of who really are the heroes and who are the villains.

**Published books:**

**A Superhero Epic Series**

Creator (2004, 2014)

He is Known as Ego (2006, 2014)

Guild Without a Name (2014)

The Galaxy Is Ours (2014)

**Non-fiction**

Jesus and the Paint on the Wall, What Do People Live For? (2012)

# List of Characters

**Matthew (James)/ Hawk** – Leader of the Guild without a Name (other aliases – Patrick Sandovel Yazi, Jason Norton, and Fredrick Malleson)

**Valerie (Janice)/ Hummel** – Member of the Guild (Second in command), procurement specialist (other aliases – Loren Malleson)

**Diana (Nyota)/ Venom** – Member of the Guild, infiltration specialist (other aliases – Vicky Hammon)

**Kyle (Khan)/ Sia** – Member of the Guild, technology specialist (other aliases – Kenji Saitou)

**Cynthia Bellows / Evergreen** – Freelance assassin and cleaner

**Sir David Lanhurst** – Billionaire philanthropist

**Alyssa Chun** – Finance of Patrick Yazi

**Felix Kendall** – International terrorist for the highest bidder

**Kurt Yazi/ Warhawk** – Superhero, worked for MI-6 and CIA. Member of The Emerald Legion in 1987 until 2002. Brother of Patrick Yazi (Mathew)

**Alicia Tarmen (Loren Melsion)** – Disciple of Joshua

**Cindy S. Owens (Samantha Brooks) / Mirage** – Disciple of Joshua

**Joshua Marks (David)** – All powerful Superhuman

**Lee Frost (Bradley Williams/Robert Williams) / Alpha** – Disciple of Joshua

**Randy Omar (Stephen Melsion)** – Disciple of Joshua

**Henry Ferguson** – Ex-Navy SEAL sniper, mercenary

**Simon Michelle** – Entrepreneur, father of the Michelle family

**Jenny Michelle** – Only child in the Michelle family

**Maria Michelle** – Mother of Jenny Michelle

**Captain Jessica Reynolds** – Mercenary, Cardigan Assassin Team Leader

**Mr. Jerry Rucker** – Malleson recruiting team instructor

**Mr. Warren Huggins** – President of the Board, Cardigan International (Weapons Technology Corporation)

**Carolyn Landings** – Director of Intelligence Analysis, Cardigan International

**Simon Brown** – Personnel Acquisitions, Cardigan International

**Ramen Connelly** – Cardigan Special Research Director, Cardigan International

**Jeremy Pines** – Appropriations Manager, Cardigan International

**Sheila Nelson** – Advertising Manager, Cardigan International

**Jonah Stiles** – (Retired) Special Advisor for Cardigan International

**Dr. Leman** – Lead Genetics Engineer and Director of Medicine, Yimen Complex, Cardigan International

Guild Without a Name, A Superhero Epic

# Contents

# Chapter One

O✦O

# A Cause

### TWA Flight 3225, January 14, 1987

Strong rays of sunlight entered the economy class compartment as Jenny cracked open the window blind. The light stung her eyes and many other passengers on the plane. She could see the mountain peaks in the distance below with a mixture of white and gray clouds covering the mountain's extreme angles and ground below. The Nepal Mountain Range seemed to extend forever along the horizon. The clear blue sky above was beautifully vast.

Jenny smiled at the site, and then frowned as many voices behind her complained about the light shining in on their interrupted slumber.

"Jenny, close the shutter; people are trying to sleep." Simon Michelle, a fairly young entrepreneur quickly whispered into her ear.

"But I want to see the snow on the pretty mountains."

Jenny disappointedly said while she rubbed her eyes with wrist and hands.

Simon grabbed his daughter's arm, gently pulled her down away from the window, and slid the blind shut. There were a few people up and about just before the end of the in flight movie, and Jenny's site seeing incident. Simon looked at his wife next to him.

"Honey, I have to use the toilet. Jenny, do you need to potty?" Maria said.

"Mommy, I want to see the snow."

"Well, we can all go to the back and look out the window after you use the toilet." Simon suggested. He slipped his socked feet into his traveling sandals neatly arranged on the floor.

"Oh, goodie." Jenny giggled and quickly clapped her hands together.

The Michelle family made their way to the back of the 747 Jumbo Jetliner. Maria went back to her seat after a while leaving Simon and Jenny looking at the mountain peaks and morning Sun. The flight was very smooth at 40,000 feet and everything was as perfect as it could be. She sat down and buckled her seatbelt out of habit. Maria looked for her headset seeing a piece of tubing sticking out from underneath her leg. She leaned to the side trying to raise her body off the headset.

A rustling sound whist by her and her head whipped back as someone ran down the aisle. Her neck and head ached with pain as she grabbed at them with her hands. "Hey!" She squealed, and then grunted.

There were screams coming from the front of the plane as another person ran by, but this time Maria protected her head keeping it away from the edge of the aisle. She looked up to see a man in a Native American Indian western style costume. The heavyset man was wearing a warrior outfit with a bandana on his head, and war paint on his face and arms.

"Get out of the way!" He yelled as he ran down the aisle.

The man quickly ran out of Maria's line of sight behind her seat. She could only see down the aisle and the lights at the rear of the compartment turning on. The curtains behind her compartment kept her from seeing what was happening, even though they were partially open.

Shortly after the lights came on, she heard many other screams. Maria looked down at her seatbelt buckle trying to undo it but hysteria on her part made her very clumsy. Terrible screams from men, women and children echoed throughout the plane as an explosion went off and the cabin decompressed. All loose objects slammed onto the ceiling for a few seconds, then slammed to the right as the plane made a hard left bank maneuver. Oxygen masks popped out of the top counters.

Maria managed to scream a little bit before the very thin air started to slowly suffocate her, even though it was more of a sensation than an abrupt reality. She grabbed the oxygen mask and frantically breathed into it as she tried to look towards the back again. The curtains were flapping sideways and to her horror a very bright light came in, near where she left her daughter and husband. The plane was losing altitude as the autopilot intentionally and aggressively told the plane to drop down below 12,000 feet causing the passengers to hold for dear life to anything permanently attached to the floor. The explosion caused the plane to bank left momentarily, but the autopilot adjusted as designed.

The vacuum of air suddenly stopped, and the plane eventually leveled off into a fixed altitude over 25,000 feet, above the dense clouds. The visibility and mountain range was the main factor in the pilot taking complete control away from the autopilot and keeping a high altitude now that cabin pressure was restored after the auto pilot was allowed to make the plane go into a dive right after the decompression, but to Maria none of the inner emergency workings of pilot decisions or procedures were important to her. She jumped out of her seat and ran to the back fearing the worst.

Warhawk stood in front of a hole double the size of the non-existent door to the rear of the plane. The hole was patched up with a reddish static looking force field. Warhawk was a superhuman working for the Central Intelligence Agency (CIA). His specialty was on counterespionage; however, his reputation as an anti-terrorist led him to travel between continents on this particular month and by chance to TWA Flight 3225. He wore mirror reflecting goggles, red, yellow and blue war paint on his face. A small silver compound bow with no visible bowstring was by his side. He knelt down next to the opening looking out into the clouds, then back towards Maria.

"Jenny! Simon!" Maria yelled as she sprinted next to him.

Several passengers were crying or silent from shock. The rest were trying to prepare for the worst; not that having a hole in the plane was bad enough, but they wrapped themselves to their chairs or tried to move away from the rear of the plane. A few passengers had broken bones from the heavy mess tables and attendants getting lifted into the air and then coming back down on the wrong spots.

Maria made it next to Warhawk and fell on her hands and knees. Her heart pounded with sorrow as she realized Simon and Jenny were no longer on the plane.

"No!" Maria screamed. "Oh, God, no!" She sobbed almost unable to breath.

Warhawk sat on the floor next to Maria and grabbed her arm. Maria instinctively hugged his arm, sobbing uncontrollably. Warhawk was Navajo by birth and was raised on a reservation most of his life. He was used to seeing people die, the good and bad at an early age during his law enforcement days, but he seemed just as devastated as Maria by the event. He did not cry or moan; he just moved slowly as if in a state of temporary shock.

"I'm so sorry." Warhawk finally said with a very heavy and compassionate voice.

He took off his goggles and stared at Maria. "I'm so sorry, I couldn't save them."

Maria finally came to grips with herself as passengers were moved forward away from the hole. Everyone left Warhawk and Maria alone out of fear or knowing Warhawk was handling the current situation with Maria.

"What happened?" Maria asked, looking up at his face,

not bothering to dry her face or wipe her runny nose.

Warhawk stared out through the hole. "There was a man named Felix Kendall, a known terrorist. I don't know how he came to be on board, because him and two other companions weren't on the passenger manifest." He paused as if visualizing the events in his head. "I recognized two of them, but it was too late, because they spotted me first. Felix knew I would not let them get away with a high jacking, so he tried to kill me and ran to the back."

Warhawk paused again, as if regretting what he was about to say. "I ran after him. He tried to grab a little girl but one of the other terrorist got in between them. Felix put a gun to the head of the girl's father. The third terrorist jumped him and kept the gun from going off, but there was a bomb around Felix's waist. The man and I assume your husband tried to stop Felix from triggering it, but they couldn't and it went off."

"Felix, Alyssa, your husband and daughter were sucked out through that hole."

Maria's eyes showed interest and disbelief. "You said there were three terrorist."

"Yes, the third terrorist took the blast so most of it went outward. He wasn't sucked out; but he jumped out after your daughter and Alyssa."

"I don't understand." Maria sat up looking at Warhawk for answers.

"I don't know what they were thinking."

"Who?"

Warhawk kept silent for a second. "The man and woman, who jumped out, were superhumans."

"So they jumped out to save Jenny?" Maria continued with her questioning.

"Yes, but they can't fly and the fall will kill them." Warhawk replied sadly.

"What if they can survive the fall?" Maria asked with a flicker of hope for her family.

"No, I'm sure they are dead now." Warhawk replied, and held his tongue; even if the man or woman could survive the fall through some miracle, her daughter would not.

"How are you so sure?"

Warhawk looked Maria in the eyes. "The man who jumped out after them was my brother."

Maria said not a word. Warhawk's eyes said it all. He loved his half brother and now he was dead. They both sat there mourning their lost.

"Sir is it safe to be near the hole?" the head stewardess asked.

"Yes, but you need to tell the Captain that she has about three hours before the energy field goes away, so I suggest she find the nearest available landing strip or at least get to a lower altitude." Warhawk calmly replied.

The stewardess froze for a second trying to regain her composure and ran her fingers up and through her hair getting most of her long loose strands neatly tucked behind her ears. "I'll let the Captain know."

Warhawk and Maria stared outside the hole for the entire duration of the flight before they made an emergency landing in Pakistan.

## 30 minutes prior to take off of flight TWA Flight 3225

Patrick Sandoval Yazi stacked baggage neatly and efficiently. He shrewdly looked at the other workers as the last load of baggage went up the tram into the cargo hull of the Boeing 747 jetliner. Alyssa Chun helped him strap in the last container of bags and instead of exiting the plane, she, Patrick and Felix Kendall went towards the front of the plane along the cargo compartments. All of the arrangements had been made and they were not noticed when they disappeared from the loading detail. Felix led the way into the cramp passages and eventually sat in a corner waiting for the plane to take off.

Patrick was of moderate height, very muscular, had greenish gray eyes and short ebony black hair trimmed all the way around his head. He sat across from Felix, next to Alyssa. Felix and Alyssa were his teammates in a world of terrorism. Yes, he was a terrorist, fighting against the oppressive governments around the world and allying himself with the governments who best served his interests. He did not see himself as a terrorist, but more like a liberator with all the skills of a professional assassin. He was a young veteran of war, but he never had been in a hostage situation where he or his finance were the hostage takers. It was not his usual type of mission, but it was a mission he volunteered at Alyssa's request. He thought about the missions Felix and him had done together and realized that this was the third mission, all the other missions he had done were with Alyssa or solo. He looked at Alyssa and felt better about being in the plane. This was to be their last mission and retirement in the name of the Liberation Front of Turkey, and a few other groups he was previously affiliated with. It was a simple takeover of the plane, where Alyssa would pilot the craft into China. It was a smoke screen as four passengers would be taken into Chinese custody as traitors, but only Felix knew the real reason for landing in China. To Patrick and Alyssa it was a very profitable mission which didn't involve killing hostages or people to make a million dollars, paid for by China with the help of the Soviet Union State Security Committee, commonly known as the KGB. It was not a conventional hijacking as they would leave the plane on Chinese territory without demanding anything, and cause an international incident in the process.

Patrick gazed at Alyssa's wonderful face and enchanting smile. He smiled himself as he thought about the planned wedding with Alyssa once the mission was completed. Her Japanese-American facial features and blue eyes was a creation made in heaven. She had the best of Japanese and American genes and it showed. Patrick was a very lucky man to have such a wonderful and beautiful woman. Alyssa had wanted to run away with him and start a new life for a very long time. After living with her for ten months, he finally had the chance to get away from his dangerous life style. The anti-government feelings he had in the past were just that now and soon he would be able to look forward to a semi bright future. After a moment of admiring his fiancée, he looked back at Felix who was now staring him in the face.

Felix's emotionless eyes and face showed nothing, but Patrick knew he was jealous, wanting Alyssa for himself. Patrick closed his eyes as if resting, and rotated his head, stretching out his neck muscles. Felix just stared at him and Alyssa. Felix met Patrick two years ago, but never really socialized with him until Alyssa came into the picture. Felix was above average height with black wavy hair. His half mixture of Spaniard and German facial traits didn't reveal a handsome and bright complexion. Instead the scars of anger and history of stress overshadowed his complexion showing off his hard and strong thick brows and brown eyes. Felix was a true anti-imperialist and was not sure where Patrick stood. His dedication to a cause whether twisted or not, was all he had to live for. In the end it was him against the world that didn't bend to his will or idea of righteousness.

The plane took off as scheduled and they hid in the baggage compartment waiting for the right time to go upstairs. They changed into casual clothes and only Felix armed himself with a handgun; while Patrick had his hunting knife. Alyssa had no weapon, but unknown to Felix, Patrick and Alyssa were far from normal. They were part of a group who were recently emerging to be called superhumans. Alyssa was very strong and could survive in very hostile environments for months without needing to eat. Patrick was much more powerful being able to increase his molecular structure and make himself a hundred times heavier than his normal weight. He was also faster and could survive in hostile environments for unknown amounts of time. The only thing Felix knew from his experience being with the couple was that they could hold off an army when it came to hand to hand combat and they didn't need a weapon to get passengers to do their bidding. It was unknown and ill-fated for everyone in the flight that Felix was a person of radical ideas which included strapping himself with explosives as a means of domination and his twisted sense of pride for his way of never being captured.

A few hours into the flight, the three went up through the service elevator and up to the rear of the plane. Felix found several unoccupied seats in the rear and casually sat down. Patrick and Alyssa also sat in empty seats and waited patiently for the plane to get closer to their desired flight path. After the in flight movie finished they got up and began their reconnaissance for potential hazards to the mission, before they would take control and redirect the plane to China.

Patrick walked down the aisle working his way to the First Class compartment. He remembered all of the faces he saw and all of the voices he heard. Almost nothing passed his superhuman senses. His sixth sense told him there was someone or something which was displaying superhuman functions or energies. A faint but familiar scent hit his nostrils as he was about to pass the kitchen area prior to Business Class. He stopped in front of the kitchen and pretended to be stretching out his arms and back.

"Can I help you Sir?" A stewardess wearing a nylon apron and holding a meal box in her hand asked.

"Yes, I was wondering if you had an extra vegetarian meal." Patrick asked as he slowly eased his way closer to the curtain separating the Economy Class from Business Class seating.

"We have a few, but did you pre-order the meals?"

"I believe so, is there a list you can look up and see. My wife made the travel arrangements." Patrick politely said while he positioned himself perfectly between the stewardess and the curtain's edge.

"Sure, let me look." She turned around to get a list in one of the many cabinets around the kitchen.

Patrick quickly parted the curtain's edge from the wall and scanned the Business Class compartment in a few seconds. He spotted the person he least wanted to see on the plane. Even though the man's head was not facing him, he knew the scent, sound of his voice, and the back of his head like if it were his own. Kurt Yazi, his brother was on board. It was a freak coincidence, worst luck ever, or sheer defiance of probability, but they were on the same plane at the same time. Hurt was no doubt trying to get a connecting flight to Bonn and then to Libya. Kurt was not on the hour old manifest they had access to, or was actively looking for him or his team, which meant Kurt was not planning on any hijacking occurring on this flight. Either way, Kurt was his brother, a superhuman, and could easily compromise their mission. He didn't sense anyone else who was out of the ordinary, in the forward compartment and upper level just prior to the cockpit.

Patrick quickly scanned the list which the stewardess brought up in front of her. In a quick glance and upside down, Patrick picked a name of a passenger who did not order a vegetarian meal.

"My name is Oliver Ham." Patrick said and tried to point to his name on the list.

"It says here you didn't order the vegetarian meal, but if you would like I can get you one." The stewardess said trying to accommodate his needs.

"It's okay, I will be fine; I need to eat meat anyways. Doctor's orders. But thank you anyways." Patrick smiled.

The stewardess smiled back and went about her business preparing the in flight meals as Patrick left the kitchen area.

Patrick quickly went back to his seat. He sat between Felix and Alyssa and whispered. "We need to abort; Warhawk is on board."

"Are you sure?" Felix asked.

"Yes, I'm sure." Patrick replied. "We need to go back to the cargo hold and ride this flight out."

Felix stared him down. "One person is not a reason for aborting. We will continue as planned. I will take care of Warhawk."

"He will not negotiate, and he's a superhuman." Patrick tried to explain.

"I don't negotiate either." Felix said and started to stand up.

"Wait, where are you going?" Alyssa grabbed Felix's wrist. "Felix, you need to listen to Patrick."

Felix turned towards Alyssa. "No, you need to listen to

me. Do you really think we will be allowed to abort this mission? We won't have any other opportunity and the people who have already given you a down payment will take it out of our skins."

Alyssa kept quiet being divided by what Felix was saying that it was too late to turn back, and Patrick who was an experienced tactician.

Felix looked back at Patrick. "Do you have any other options? If not, then I suggest you follow my lead." He said and waited for a reply.

Patrick was thinking of options, but none of them involved anything short of knocking his brother out, which he knew would be very difficult to do without possibly hurting passengers or damaging the plane.

Felix turned around and walked down the aisle seeing that Patrick had nothing.

Alyssa nervously looked at Patrick waiting to see what he was going to do. She didn't understand why he didn't tell Felix Kurt was his brother, but maybe that wouldn't have mattered in Felix's eyes. Her long black hair draped over her left eye, slightly covering up her worried face.

Patrick held her hand. "Stay here. Whatever you do, do not attack my brother."

Alyssa understood and kissed him. "Be careful."

Patrick quickly walked down the right aisle. Half way towards the Business Class entrance, Patrick spotted Felix on the left aisle of the plane. Patrick thought about maybe letting Felix try something and his brother would take him down, but even that didn't seem right to him. He would get caught ad people might still get hurt, but his options were getting narrower as Felix was totally focused to his front and did not see Patrick on the opposite aisle. Patrick smelled Warhawk's scent, but it would have been too strong for him to sense it from this distance; unless Warhawk was not towards the front anymore and closer to the middle of the plane. Patrick saw Warhawk come out from a toilet stall along the left aisle and stop in his tracks as he spotted Felix ten meters away.

Felix lost his chance for a surprise attack and stood there a little confused as to what to do next. Warhawk took a step towards Felix and then noticed Patrick on the right side of the plane. Felix pulled out a 9mm Caliber automatic pistol with a miniature silencer and fired four bullets at Warhawk. Warhawk almost instantly took his eyes off of Patrick, placed his right leg back to take the knockback and raised his left wrist watch into the path of the bullets.

The silver watch seemed to blow up as bright blue light flashed out of it once and a light blue force field the shape and size of a small Gladiatorial shield stopped three of the bullets in mid air, with the mushroomed fragments falling on the carpeted floor. The first shot however, did hit Warhawk in the left shoulder near the arm. The round entered his body but didn't penetrate very much as it lodged itself an inch or two inside his muscle, with blood naturally coming out like a nose bleed. Felix stopped shooting and fled towards the back of the plane, stashing away the gun in his jacket as he ran down the aisle.

Warhawk's force shield disappeared once Felix lowered

his weapon. War paint instantly appeared on his face and a miniature silver bow eight inches long came out of his right wrist band, clinging to his wrist as he ran. The round in his shoulder was pushed outside of his body as he ran after Felix, with the bleeding slowing down dramatically. Patrick ran back down the aisle, parallel to Felix. Passengers that were awake and saw the incident screamed or just got out of the way. Patrick had to jump over several passengers and land on his feet and hands twice as he ran towards the back.

Alyssa intently watched Simon and Jenny who were in the rear hoping they would go back to their seats. The attendants that normally stayed in the rear were out and about in the forward galley. She got up and moved near them. She thought about Felix and the homemade bomb he wore on his waist. If the belt went off or anything happened that could damage the plane, she would be in trouble by standing around with no seat belt. Alyssa went to the window next to Simon and Jenny. The exit door was one window down from the one they were looking through. Simon noticed Alyssa move into their personal space and looked around. He looked for a boyfriend or something that might be causing Alyssa to come within inches of them.

'There was plenty of room in front of the door, so why was she rubbing elbows with him and Jenny?'

Alyssa saw that the best place to be if something happened, besides being in a passenger seat, was the spot they were standing on. The low ceiling created by the overhang compartment and the rear most wall connected to the rear seats provided some available foot and hand holds, and protection from flying projectiles. She perceived Simon seemed to be uncomfortable about her presence.

Alyssa looked at Simon with Jenny in between them. "Oh, excuse me. I didn't realize you two were here." She said almost half asleep.

Simon and Jenny stepped away from the window.

She looked down at Jenny, who was wearing cute green overalls and a white long sleeve cotton shirt. She knelt down to Jenny's eye level and made a wide smile showing off two beautiful rows of white teeth. "You have a beautiful daughter." She complimented them both.

Simon placed his hands on top of Jenny's shoulders. "She takes after her mother." Simon replied without a smile.

Alyssa looked awake now and stood up as she looked at Simon. "I'm sorry, my name Tia, I just woke up and had to stretch my legs."

"Oh, we understand. I'm Simon." Simon said a little more at case.

"Hi Simon." Alyssa said and held out her hand. Simon shook her hand but kept the other hand on Jenny.

"And what is your name, little one?" Alyssa innocently asked.

Jenny giggled and turned around hugging her father. "Her name is Jenny." Simon answered for her.

"Boy, you're really shy." Alyssa smiled and bowed her

head down to Jenny's head.

Jenny looked at Alyssa with a big smile. "I'm not supposed to talk to strangers."

"That's good, you shouldn't talk to strangers, but that is when you are by yourself or other children. It's okay to talk to strangers if your mom or dad is with you." Alyssa said as she kneeled again down to Jenny's eye level.

"It's okay Jenny, I'm here." Simon reinforced Alyssa's statement.

"So what were you two doing?" Alyssa changed the subject.

"We were looking at the snow." Jenny happily replied.

"Yea, but the dark clouds are starting to cover the peaks." Simon added.

"Really?" Alyssa thought quickly. "You know there is a very tall mountain you can see on the other side there." She lied and pointed to the right side of the plane.

She wasn't sure where Felix, Patrick or Warhawk were on the plane, but she knew if she could get Simon and Jenny near the empty seats she had occupied, then they would be somewhat safer.

"Really?" Jenny's eyes widen with joy. "Oh, daddy, can we go see?"

Alyssa heard a very faint thumping sound and turned towards the front. Her face tensed with seriousness. The silencer muffled the load bang, but there was still a loud thumping sound, and she could not mistake it for anything else. She kept her eyes towards the front.

"Okay, let's go see." Simon agreed to Alyssa's relief.

Simon waited for Alyssa to lead the way, but she moved slowly, her attention was towards the front of the plane. Simon turned his attention to the front also, wondering what Alyssa was looking at. He heard someone scream, saying to get out of the way and saw Felix sprinting towards him.

Jenny was half way to the other side when Alyssa realized Felix was on a rampage and fleeing for his life. She forcefully grabbed Simon and ran off after Jenny. Simon tripped as one of his sandals rubbed on the carpet too fast, curled up and twisted his ankle. Alyssa was almost pulled down by Simon's weight and unexpected motion, but kept her footing. Jenny turned around and saw her father on the floor. She naturally ran towards him wanting to help him up. Felix was almost on top of Simon when he slightly changed his direction straight for Jenny who was next to Simon and Alyssa now.

Alyssa saw Felix's fanatical expression on his face as he drew his gun out from underneath his jacket. She leaped at Jenny, tackling her to the floor, which left Simon in Felix's alternate path.

Felix grabbed at Simon's arm, but ended up almost falling past him as the momentum of his sprint messed with his footing. The raised attendant seat took most of this weight, and he bounced off and landed on Simon's legs. Simon was terrified and kicked at Felix, but Felix instantly jumped on top of him and placed the hand gun barrel to Simon's temple.

Jenny was screaming as she saw her father in danger. Patrick had arrived by Jenny and Alyssa's side only to draw out his knife. Felix struggled to get up with Simon, but was only able to get to his knees. He saw the drawn out knife and eyed Patrick's motives. Patrick did not need to have a gun in his hand, the knife was just as deadly even though it was a one shot deal if he threw the weapon.

"What are you doing!" Felix said loudly over the screams and panic, trying to figure out why Patrick didn't help him and fight Warhawk.

"Let him go!" Warhawk chimed into the conversation.

"Do as he says Felix." Patrick said, knowing Felix was totally out of control and wanted blood, even if it was his own.

Felix pulled Simon closer to him and also towards the rear window and door. Felix didn't think twice about his options and grabbed at his explosive belt's safety mechanism. Patrick didn't notice the deadly weapon until it was too late. Felix had dropped his gun muzzle away from Simon's head, but kept a grip on Simon's neck with his other arm.

Patrick was completely outraged that this man he once thought was sound minded was acting like a complete blood thirsty killer. Patrick took his opportunity and threw his knife at Felix's hand. The knife point hit its mark, but it was too late as the momentum of the throw and impact pushed Felix's hand into the belt the wrong way. In an instant, the explosion of the C4 composite expanded to engulf anything close to it. Patrick instinctively stepped forward in front of Alyssa and Jenny. The concussion and debris of the explosion seemed to have no effect on Patrick's body defeating any kind of knockback, but it did shred his clothes, and the rear kitchen and latrine compartment doors and cabinets. The blast created a two man size hole where the door existed and the vacuum sucked out Felix's and Simon's remains of intact flesh and bones. Alyssa and Jenny received some secondary fragments because of Patrick's stance, but the suction flung them towards the hole. Alyssa horrified, tried to hold tight to Jenny, but failed miserably. Jenny flew out of the plane, as Alyssa grabbed on to Patrick's ankle.

She was in pain and terrified as Jenny's face left her view. Patrick stood in a fixed stance and reached for Alyssa, but to his disbelief Alyssa let go of him and followed Jenny outside of the plane. Just then, a red glowing energy field encompassed the hole, and pressure was restored to the cabin. Warhawk's body came back down to the floor, off of the ceiling as the jetliner was trying to level off from the extreme drop in altitude.

Patrick quickly stepped forward almost on top of the energy field, and turned his head toward his brother. Patrick's eyes were full of regret and anguish as he jumped through the energy field almost collapsing it and endangering the aircraft a second time. They had the same father, and even though both their mothers were dead, it was saddening to know that Kurt would have to explain to their father what had happened to Patrick. Patrick straightened his body and fell like a missile towards small dark figures in the distance. He quickly caught up to Alyssa who was feverishly holding Jenny. Alyssa had hopelessly and illogically attempted mouth to mouth in mid air, as the lack of air and Jenny's already limp dead body only gave Alyssa a deep wound in her soul knowing she couldn't save her.

Patrick expertly slowed down and grabbed Alyssa from behind. The morning Sun penetrated the cloud cover revealing Jenny's pale face, frozen skin, and motionless eyes. Alyssa turned to meet Patrick's eyes. She knew it was hopeless, Jenny died upon exiting the plane, with the fatal damage done to her body by the edge of the hole on the plane and the attitude's environment.

Alyssa was so beautiful even in the horror of the moment. Patrick quickly kissed her as they fell towards the dark clouds below. Alyssa released Jenny and embraced her fiancé, passionately kissing him back.

Jenny seemed to float away and disappear as they entered dark clouds. Patrick and Alyssa tragically enjoyed each other's exchange of kisses for what seemed an eternity in the dark cold rushing air and water vapor. The darkness faded as they exited the lower cloud cover. They could see the ground in the far distance, but it was awkward because the snow hid the real features of the mountain ridges and valleys. Patrick's keen sixth sense was screaming at him. He concentrated and saw that they were heading towards the side of the mountain. It then occurred to him that they might be able to survive the fall if they could use the slope of the mountain to their advantage.

The rushing air made it impossible to talk to Alyssa audibly, so he quickly maneuvered her to face him by turning her and raping his legs around her waist, freeing up his hands. He quickly signed his intentions.

Alyssa understood the chopped up sign language due to the air and movement interference, and she replied by nodding and kissing Patrick quickly. There might have been a possibility of slowing down rate of speed as they fell, but time was against them and since they couldn't generate enough drag or decrease they density, the options didn't come to Patrick or Alyssa's train of thought.

Patrick grabbed Alyssa's hands and let go of his leg lock around her waist. He tried to position himself on the bottom so that once he made contact with the snow covered ground, he would initiate the roll and hopefully Alyssa would use him as a buffer and also roll along with him. The slope of the mountain might be enough so that he and Alyssa might be able to roll over and over until the force of terminal velocity was dispersed among their bodies and ground. It was a crazy idea and all logic or rational physics pointing towards failure could not have taken away Patrick's hope that they would see another day.

The freezing air on their exposed skin and clothing numbed Alyssa's body, but it angered Patrick. The cold air did not harm Patrick, but he knew that it could severely hurt Alyssa in the long term. But first thing first, the ground was coming quickly and he had to time it perfectly. He increased his grip and decreased his grip on Alyssa's hands counting down from three to let her know when he planned to roll with the ground.

Patrick's timing was acutely perfect and a sudden push on the side of his back turned into a push to his front side to include Alyssa's body slightly pushing against his body as they rolled with the punch of the ground. They miraculously hit the ground with their sides facing the slope so that when they rolled, they rolled sideways instead of head over heal. The initial impact was buffered for the moment, but the constant tumbling was relentless along with gravity. They ended up going head over heal after fifty meters and broke physical contact shortly afterwards. Patrick's arm ached in pain as it broke, which was a feat that only happened once in his life when he fought a charging rhino in Africa. The snow had helped greatly in softening the impact, but large rock formations seemed to penetrate the deep snow and inflict physical harm on both of them.

Patrick increased his body density weighing a few tons and finally came to a stop on a leveled section of the slope. He didn't make himself heavier earlier knowing that if he did his weight would crush Alyssa if he had rolled on top of her. The only advantage of increasing his density was that he would be able to take more damage which he did once Alyssa was not with him anymore. He stood up and scanned the area for Alyssa. He saw her still sliding down the mountain side fifty feet away. He decreased his body density to normal and painfully raced after her. It was another fifty meters before Alyssa's motionless body came to a halt. It wasn't snowing, but the dark cloud cover made visibility difficult as if in the late evening, but Patrick's senses were as keen as ever having no problem seeing her body features in the distance.

Patrick painfully caught up to Alyssa who was on her back. Her leg was contorted with her left foot underneath her lower back. Half frozen blood was present in both ears, and nostrils. Patrick tenderly checked for internal damage, as he checked for a response, "Alyssa, can you hear me?"

Alyssa opened her eyes, and felt numb all over the lower parts of her body. She strained to pickup her head, but failed wretchedly. "I can't feel my hands and legs."

Patrick felt massive damage to her vertebrates. Alyssa was paralyzed from the neck down as far as he could tell and what she just confirmed. "Your vertebrates around the C5 and T1 are damaged. You can't feel your broken bones because you are paralyzed," Patrick sadly replied knowing she was much tougher than a normal human, but her ability to take punishment only allowed her to keep from instantly dying on impact or in the air.

Alyssa stared into Patrick's dark eyes, "I don't want to die slowly."

Patrick stared deep into her tearing eyes. "I'm so sorry my love. It's all my fault."

"Don't blame yourself; I should have protected you better." Alyssa joked with a very weak smile.

Patrick sat next to her and tried to cover her head from the elements with his half shredded shirt.

Alyssa saw the pain and torture he was enduring to stay with her in the middle of nowhere. "You need to leave me."

Patrick looked at her and gently picked her up cradling her in his arms. "I will never leave you my beloved wife." The broken bone in his arm was mended to a hairline fracture, but painful still. He endured the pain for Alyssa's sake and walked slowly down the slope. He used the entire surface space of his arms and extended fingers to cradle her; supporting her legs, back, and head.

Alyssa didn't protest, to him calling her his wife, and to him taking her even though she was reducing his chances of surviving by caring for her. The movement of her body was also doing more damage to her, but it didn't matter to her. She did not expect to live for long, unless there was a trauma team ten meters away, she would die in an hour or maybe minutes.

Patrick kept an eye on the broken bones to make sure he did not inflict more damage or cause her to go into shock. After a quarter of a mile, Alyssa started to cough intermittently. Patrick walked another quarter of a mile, but stopped once Alyssa started to cough blood. He gently placed her on the ground but kept her in a sitting position.

Alyssa could barely speak now. "I can't breathe."

Patrick knew even though she could normally hold her breathe for over an hour, blood may have been filling her lung or lungs or something else was wrong, but it didn't matter because he could do nothing about her inability to breathe. "I can't do anything." he said despairingly.

"You didn't kill her, but don't let her death be for nothing." Alyssa said. "Now, kill me." She pleaded.

Patrick looked at her, hesitant to grant her request. "I will always love you my beloved." He placed both his hands on the sides of her head and kissed her. In an instant, he twisted her head with superhuman strength and broke her neck.

Patrick groaned as he embraced his future wife and screamed a violent scream of anger. His scream echoed throughout the valley louder than a wolf's howl on a clear summer night.

Patrick wept for a long time.

He stood up and cradled Alyssa's body once again, and made his way down to a remote abandoned climber's staging camp. His sixth sense of direction, scouting, or local awareness was not failing him. Ten hours later, he entered a small village. The Indian inhabitants were more of less receptive of the stranger and the frozen dead woman.

Patrick did not speak a word, and instead signed to them, but ended up using hand gestures as no one was knowledgeable in sign language. It didn't matter to him though, because they didn't know English and he didn't know their Newrai dialect. The village leaders agreed to aid Patrick and help him bury Alyssa. Patrick did not plan on staying long. His broken bone and other minor injuries were all healed before he took a step into their village. The only thing that gave him constant pain was his broken heart and remorse for being a past participant to many deaths, especially Jenny, hcr father, and his own true love.

He stayed in the village for a few days and left with painful knowledge of where his finance was buried. Patrick took a long hike through the mountains, six months later he stepped into the city streets of Kathmandu. He made his way to Bangladesh, where he procured a ride to Port Sudan. He walked or hitchhiked to Cairo where he established a business for helping the hearing impaired using computer digital and physical platforms and programs.

His three year sabbatical gave him a lot of time to reflect on his future. He spent many nights with images of Alyssa, Jenny, Kurt, and Simon as background for many nightmares and regrets. Patrick decided he would not speak unless his life required it; which helped him not have to speak to people about his feelings and history. He used some of his fronts from the past to erase all trace of his identity, in particular any voice, facial, dental, and finger print recognition files or documents. It was not as hard as he expected since he was thought to have been deceased. The first Super Artificial Intelligence (SAI) named Loki, in the superhero group The Emerald Legion, was fed false information from the source. If the SAI did its job, all other identification computers or agencies would follow its lead. No one knew or could have come close to identifying Patrick except the few people who still lived, like his older brother Kurt.

He and his brother did not see eye to eye on many things, but for almost two decades, he missed his brother and wished he had listened to Kurt more often. He kept watch over Kurt from a distance, and thought about one day revealing himself to him. Unfortunately, Kurt never saw his brother again as time passed and Kurt died while working with the Special Investigation Agency (SIA).

Patrick's new identity was now Jason Norton, a mute who was wealthy from his own business which included translation of services to and from brail, and digital media as well. His half American Indian traits were very faint and he blended in well with a large number of international tourists and business people. It brought in a steady legitimate income while in Egypt, which in a few years, his company expanded into other African and a few

European countries. In a span of fifteen years, Jason, was making a seven figure income.

The problem was that Jason was bored of the simple and monotonous work which gave him fulfillment to a point and sometimes a little bit of excitement. He was very generous giving to charity and many causes for children, women, and families, but something was missing. The days of thievery, cloak and dagger were in the past, but not forgotten. He missed those times and thought about how he could get both. He took his time and planned out a network of locations and targets. He was a person with a purpose. His purpose was not for himself, it was to help others. The wealthy rich were for the most part too wealthy.

The excess of wealth was his excuse to distribute among the needy. He understood that many people did in fact work hard for their position in the upper class and had a right to enjoy what they were blessed with, but it did not matter to him if those super wealthy lost a small portion of that wealth. He would steal from the people that could afford to be stolen from, which meant that the crooked wealthy people where by default the prime targets. This included the establishments of the humanities and items of the super elite with private art collections and facilities.

# Chapter Two

O❖O

# The New Family

## Yimen Research Center, Elyria, Ohio, November 7, 2006

Joshua's stomach ached with pain. The constant flow of drugs in his system was eating away at him. He laid helpless, bound hands and legs to his bed with very thick nylon belts. His head was not strapped down, less he had to turn to the side and vomit. Tears ran down his unshaven face and ears, feeling so alone in the prison he vowed to destroy. His black hair was dirty from many days of neglect, and but there was no noticeable neglect to his semi muscular body. The room was sterile with the only piece of furniture being a specially made bed, which was welded to the metallic floor. Four months had passed and no word on his wife and daughter. The Cardigan foundation made many promises and his only shred of comfort he possessed was his hope that they would keep at least one of them.

He thought of Jonah Stiles, the only person to have treated him with respect and in a weird kind of way – some kindness. Joshua could not forget Jonah's sadden expression on his face during their last encounter. Jonah was in his late forties and a widower. He knew Jonah couldn't speak what was in his heart with two telepaths hovering over them both as Joshua told him "one day no one would be safe." The impression of Jonah's reaction toward Joshua was ignored by the telepaths as if his and Joshua's situation was futile. Jonah knew Joshua would get his revenge and he was a simple pawn in a game of deadly experimentation on superhumans.

Joshua was a mentally gifted superhuman before being recruited by the foundation. He underwent a special experiment which enhanced his mental abilities to great proportions. It seemed to be the breakthrough the foundation was looking for until Joshua discovered their true intentions - intentions of harvesting his mental abilities for use in wars and government takeovers. He conspired to expose the foundation, but instead caused his wife and daughter to be abducted and used against him. He was now a helpless Guinea Pig to further their experiments.

Joshua breathed deeply and calmed down knowing the daily routine and what the monstrous doctors were planning to do that day. He was getting stronger even though liters of anti-psychotic drugs suppressed his mental powers. The foundation was using untested drugs which had already killed twenty-three test victims and he knew it was a matter of time before he became one of those statistics.

There were two hidden security cameras in the room, but it didn't matter to Joshua because his great escape plan started in the room but was invisible to the trained eye. Joshua concentrated on the drugs in his entire body and telekinetically separated their chemical bond and pushed a good portion of them to his stomach. He hoped his timing was right, but wasn't sure since his internal sense of time was somewhat out of whack. The drugs would slowly digest back into his blood stream and all the effort he put into moving the toxic substances would be wasted.

The sound of a key turning the lock tumblers to his door could be heard in the silent room. The latch on his door sprung out and the door opened to his relief. Two medical technicians and two telepaths entered the room. One of the technicians pushed in a heavy steel wheelchair. His arms, legs, and back muscles strained as he parked the chair next to Joshua's bed.

Joshua could feel the telepaths invade his mind. It sickened him as they took apart his memories, but kept them from seeing what he was up to. The telepaths only saw his efforts to comfort a non-existent ulcer, and a stomach full of blood.

One of the telepaths smiled wickedly as he saw Joshua's mental and intestinal suffering.

The first technician looked at Joshua's pupils with a pen light, and then checked his vitals on a small scanner placed on his chest, "He is still sedated."

"Give him 1,000 milligrams." The second telepath commanded.

The technician looked back at him a little afraid.

"But, he's sedated."

"I don't care. Give him 1,000 milligrams." The telepath unsympathetically replied.

The technician's face showed concern, but fear of the telepath overcame him and he did as instructed. The other technician prepared the chair and started to untie Joshua's binds as 1,000 milligrams of Lithium was intravenously injected into Joshua's body.

Joshua felt the drug burn in his veins as he had a mild allergic reaction to it. He felt very weak, but managed to keep from passing out.

The four men took Joshua out into the hallway and through a maze of corridors. Joshua could barely keep awake as they entered an elevator and went down many levels. He did not need to stay awake to know where they were taking him, but more so to keep the drugs in his stomach at bay.

The five men finally made it to a very large white empty room except at the center. Five chairs were placed in a semicircle facing two small medical mobile tables. Two men and a woman sat on three of the chairs while a middle-aged man in a white doctor's coat waited by the medical tables.

Joshua was wheeled in front of the two medical tables facing the five chairs. The tables looked like tall square plastic night stands with drawers and electronic gadgetry on the upper portion of the tables. Black tubular prongs were connected to Joshua's chest and head from the tables with great care by the technicians. The two escorting telepaths sat down on the empty chairs while the doctor examined Joshua's vital signs.

"Welcome back Joshua." Dr. Wood said with a trace of sick pleasure in his callous voice.

Joshua didn't reply as he conserved his strength and ignored the wicked doctor. His mind strained with apathy and uncertainty, but his inner soul focused on one thing. He had to scan the minds of the people in front of him without any of them knowing what he was doing. The telepaths before him were experienced in probing for thoughts, but he was hoping they would underestimate his mastery of telepathy. He was getting stronger every day since he successfully controlled the drugs in his system with telekinesis and controlled his physical body. It was ironic that the drugs used to suppress his powers also helped in camouflaging his ability to overcome their effects.

The interrogation was about to begin. All five telepaths would invade his mind and start taking it apart, trying to figure out how he achieved the ability to draw the life force from living beings. Joshua's ability to draw power from a living being was not great, but the fact that it could be done was something no superhuman was able to do except for him. Joshua had not revealed any secrets and the only reason the foundation knew about his special ability was through the interrogation of his wife.

It had been eight months since he developed the unique ability, but his drug induced imprisonment had kept him from knowing his true potential. It really didn't matter to Joshua if he could suck the life out of living cells. He kept his ability a mystery in order to delay certain death for him and his family. There was hope in him, perhaps hope for a miracle when he and his family would be free. He yearned to know about the safety of his wife and daughter. Time was running out for them. Soon he would become useless to the foundation and then his family would certainly be killed.

He felt so helpless knowing he only had one chance to find out how his family faired. A deep probe into one of the minds in the room would alert the telepaths that the drugs were not doing their job. Joshua would have to get surface thoughts from the doctors who weren't able to protect themselves from his mind scan. He would have less than a minute to scan a doctor before the telepaths started to invade his own mind at full strength.

He sent a mental image into Dr. Leman's mind, not once letting his right hand know what his left hand was doing. Dr. Leman heard one of the technicians next to him ask him a question.

"Doctor, where is Joshua's wife and daughter now?"

The doctor looked at the technician a little confused. He instinctively thought about the answer and why the technician had asked such a question.

"What did you ask me?" Dr. Leman replied, as the technician looked at him dumbfounded, having never said a word to Dr. Leman.

It was all Joshua needed. Surface thoughts came up in Dr. Leman's mind. Joshua saw what he feared the most and heartbreaking agony came over him. He saw and heard a conversation between Dr. Leman and the foundation president of the board, Mr. Huggins.

'You need to make sure Joshua never finds out his wife and daughter are dead.' Mr. Huggins said.

Joshua lost control for a few seconds and the lead telepath felt his horrifying pain. "Something is wrong! Knock him out!" the telepath yelled.

The five telepaths attacked Joshua's subconscious with unyielding fury.

Joshua felt intense nausea and dizziness, but the anguish of the death of his true loves kept him from falling unconscious. He dug deep into his soul and lashed out, sending a mental blot of confusion into four of the telepaths.

Dr. Wiess's voice came over the loud speaker from the control room. "Do you have him under control?" he asked, standing in front of the alarm ready to call for reinforcements.

"We have him under control." The lead telepath replied not knowing his companions were temporarily stunned.

Joshua quickly recovered from the massive mental attack and concentrated on the lead telepath, breaking his mental hold. Joshua dug even deeper into his soul with all his might and focused on Dr. Weiss in the control room. He could not visually see the doctor, but it didn't matter since he could see his mental thoughts like a ship in the dark to a beaconing lighthouse. Dr. Weiss' body collapsed on the floor as every cell in his body was completely drained of life.

The two technicians in the control room trembled in horror as they too felt their life force being sucked out while they witnessed Dr. Weiss' physical body literally disintegrate into a puddle of liquid dead flesh mixed in with carbon and bone fragments. Joshua absorbed the power from the three life forces in the control room and instinctively enhanced all of his powers tenfold. Joshua didn't understand how he absorbed so much power so quickly, but he wasn't thinking about anything at that point except revenge on his enemies.

He mentally attacked the telepaths, technicians, and Dr. Leman in the main room paralyzing them into a vegetative state. They all fell on the metallic floor lifeless. Joshua screamed in pain and anger. All of his restraints broke apart with a quick telekinetic jolt of sheer anger. He lunged forward off his chair falling on his hands and knees. He sobbed and moaned for a few minutes as he ended up on his back. Every memory of his beloved wife and daughter flashed before him which fueled his thrust for retribution.

He stared at the ceiling after regaining his composure. He sat up and sucked out the life force essence from all eight people around him and watched them physically melt away into small puddles of black liquid. He felt his mind expand beyond the room and encompass the complex. The minds of everyone in the complex where his to see effortlessly. His clear voidance raced from one mind to another, seeing their memories, emotions and subconscious thoughts.

In an instant, he knew all the secrets and life experiences of over 200 people. Then his mind stepped into an astral plain of existence. The burning rage and thrust for vengeance vanished in the mist of absolute knowledge. Joshua saw the past, present and millions of possible futures. He could see all, but barely understood a fraction of the visions. Time seemed to stop for him as he tried to make sense of it all. The visions seemed so real and he felt the emotions each person had at that moment for each vision. Sorrow, happiness, nervousness, confidence, resentment, pride, love, desire, apathy, humility, good and evil were extensions of the people he saw. The more he concentrated, the more the visions started to overlap each other. It wasn't long before he jumped from one vision to another aimlessly in time.

He attempted to come back to the present, but found himself lost in a montage of information which kept pouring into his mind. He was going insane or perhaps was on the brink of losing his individuality forever. Joshua reached out and caught the vision which he knew was his alone; the vision of his beautiful wife and four year old daughter. His love for them prevailed and the vision of them was all he saw after a while.

Sarah was playing with their baby daughter in the bedroom. He saw the love in both their eyes and understanding came to him.

Joshua opened his eyes and came back to the present. The puddles of liquid flesh in the room didn't rot as normal. There was no scent from the lifeless microorganisms on the remains of the people he had killed without mercy.

"I'm sorry Sarah." Joshua said and covered his face with his hands and wept.

Joshua laid back down after a while and thought about what to do now. His powers were magnificent, but power was not enough to do what he knew was right. He concentrated on the visions of time again, but this time he was ready. He used the vision of his family as a starting point and ending point. He looked into the thoughts and history of all the people in the complex. Once he was satisfied with the information he was looking for, her started to slowly absorb part of everyone's life force in the complex according to their capacity without killing them. The boost of power was practically infinite and his understanding grew in likewise fashion.

He looked into the future and saw trillions of possible futures. He knew he could change the world anyway he wanted it to be in a blink of an eye. He could create and destroy anything. He could control everyone for eternity if he so wished. He was all powerful, and all knowing. He was also Joshua. A human with a soul, one out of many other souls. He saw the life which he loved too precious for him to control, so he chose a future for the human race. He would not control people, but he would guide them into a future which they could live as free and peaceful as possible.

Joshua saw the earth destroyed a billion times and a billion times he saw evil prevail. Yet there were a billion more times when Earth became a guiding light for not only the human race, but the galaxy. He would not alter the past, but would alter the future. He saw a change in the timelines for five people, but after investigating why it occurred in the past and future he allowed it to happen. It was a part of destiny which he embraced knowing that he would find a new family in the distant future so for his sake and his future family he allowed the time travel incident which would occur in a hundred years and had already occurred. He saw the world needing heroes to fight for justice and peace. He chose four separate forces of good to fight for Earth and the galaxy. He started with the four superhumans at the complex.

Joshua had to ensure justice was done and decided to make an example of the complex. He found fourteen people who were innocent of the atrocities committed in the complex and brought hell itself to over two hundred people who worked and lived within the complex. He created mental illusions which were so real to the victims that they all suffered a terrifying mental death. He then triggered the silent alarms altering the special security forces the foundation had in the area that the complex was under attack.

Joshua waited for the right time and mentally forced the truth about the complex into the fourteen survivors. Four of them were superhumans. The others were innocent workers or patients. Those humans he teleported away from the complex all across the continent, giving them a means to hide and survive so that they could live a semi normal human life. He did not teleport the four superhumans, because his plan was to make them independent and connect them as a family.

The first superhuman was Randy Omar, a wiry man in his late twenties standing a little over six feet. His sandy blond hair, military-style haircut, and muscular build showed evidence of some previous military experience. The second superhuman was an African-American, Alicia Tarmen. Her very long braided hair, beautiful face, and slender body could have easily given her a fruitful career as a super model. The third superhuman was an athletic looking blue eyed teenager, named Lee Frost. The youth's composure, however, was not like any other teen, but more like someone who had lived half a century. His dark brown hair was also styled after an Army Ranger -a high and tight, and his physical demeanor seemed to be as in the middle of extensive combat training. The last superhuman, Cindy Owens, was a teenage girl with short golden flowing hair and violet eyes, who seemed to be the youngest of the four and probably the most naïve as well. Joshua connected all four superhumans together with telepathy and had a teleconference in their minds.

Only the four appeared facing each other as in a huddle in the middle of an average garden on a mid cloudy day. Joshua wanted them to see each other for the first time so that they would have proper introductions considering the present circumstance. The four seemed bewildered by the conference, and at a loss of what to say or do, but the silence was broken by the eldest in the group.

*Why us, Joshua?* Randy asked without elaborating.

Joshua spoke amid them, *'All four of you are not responsible for the atrocities this place has committed. All of you are pure in heart and only victims of deception. The four of you are special with superhuman abilities, which can be used for good. I have seen the future and know that each one of you must live to fulfill what I call destiny.'*

*'And what if I don't believe in destiny?'* Alicia asked.

A faint mental smile could be felt as Joshua replied, *'Destiny is what you make of it. Some of you will do things that are far from saintly, but believe this: You are free for now. They will eventually come for you and some of you may die. I have given each one of you added abilities, which will help you in your quest to survive in a world full of evil and hope. Go into the world, fight injustice, and live as best you can to the fullest with love and happiness. Destiny is being fulfilled as we speak whether you believe in it or not.'*

*'Where do you fit in all of this?'* Lee asked.

*'I have powers beyond comprehension, but I will not force my absolute will on the human race. I will be around when the world needs me most. If you need me, call on me when the time is right and I will help you. Consider yourselves as brothers and sisters. Should you meet each other in the future, remember that no matter the circumstance, you can and must trust each other with your lives, for you are all one family now...'*

*'They will be here soon to see this place disappear before their very eyes. I will show them the power they have been searching for all this time. Now, quickly leave this place and be free before they arrive.'* Joshua concluded the mental conference as the images each person saw and heard slowly faded away.

Cindy did not say a word during the conference, but somehow everyone in the group knew each other's voices, history, and superhuman abilities. At the time the conference ended, Cindy was outside of building G and took to the air, flying as fast as her powers would allow her to get away from the complex.

Randy and Alicia were in the lobby of building C, when they decided to leave together with Alicia carrying Randy as she also flew away from the complex. Lee was still in his room at the end of the conference, but he soon saw that Joshua had opened or unlocked all the doors leading to the lobby of Building B. He quickly ran outside ignoring the many dead bodies of workers and scientists. Lee could sense everything around him as if he were some super living area tracking device or radar. He ran across the grass and dirt only to see his tracks disappear behind him. He knew he was not erasing the tracks, but he could see them being erased. He thought about it for a second and concluded that Joshua was helping him escape without leaving a trace of his presence. He reached the perimeter fence line and heard a piercing roar of rushing trains or machinery behind him. Lee instantly glanced back and saw the dozen or so buildings in the complex get tossed up into the atmosphere in a span of a second or two, like a futuristic teleporter going haywire on the buildings to include the underground structures.

Lee jumped over the fifteen foot non-working electrified fence and into the trees, but stopped at a vantage point to see what was going to happen next. Lee was not afraid of being caught, not because Joshua was helping him, but because he knew his powers would allow him to escape with ease now that he was in the forest. Either way, he wanted to know who might be following him in the future, so he stuck around for the bad guys. It was not long before Lee got some answers. Helicopters stormed the area with three landing inside the perimeter and four others circling about. Lee kept still in his position and scanned the people exiting the helicopters on the ground. His enhanced telescopic night vision allowed him to clearly see minute details to include name tags. However, there were no markings of any kind on the equipment or uniforms used by the security response force.

A man in his mid forties walked up to the main building entry way, but all that was present of the building was a massive hole in the ground extending into where the lower levels once used to be. A much older woman in her seventies followed the man, acting like an assistant, carrying a large kit bag strapped to her left shoulder.

Lee had super hearing, but could not hear the conversation about 100 meters away among the background helicopter noise and movement of the security guards scouting the area. He did not really need to hear the conversation exactly, because he could see the man's very concerned facial expressions, and the woman's confused face for the first part of the conversation, and then also turned to concern. The dialogue did not last very long, and the pair left the area as quickly as they came. Lee felt very conflicted. He had a desire to go and kill those people in the clearing, but knew that if he did, then the foundation would know there were survivors besides Joshua and the others would be hunted down. The pain of his entire family being murdered was very heavy, but he was at peace at the same time. Joshua must have given him strength or something. He was not sure what it was, but then he looked at his hands holding on to a tree branch. Just as the tree had grown to maturity, he needed to grow and maybe then he will get his justice or at least be strong enough to forgive. Heavy machinery arrived an hour later, and started to fill-in the holes and destroy the remaining fence line. Lee by this time had moved away from the area at a snail's pace and was only three hundred meters into the woods in that hour, before he started to jump from tree to tree. Lee didn't know he could fly until he was flying like Peter Pan in between the trees. Joshua must have given him the ability, but he didn't stop to figure why or how. He quickly got a mile away and then soared through the sky brushing along the tree tops heading south until sunrise. Lee had a photographic memory and kept all the events and faces he saw that night deeply guarded in his mind.

Joshua saw every move made by Lee, and the foundation personnel. He knew that the fourteen survivors would not be hunted because they would be considered dead, and their new lives would provide a lasting freedom without them looking over their shoulders. Unfortunately, Joshua also knew that the four superhumans he had just made into a family would not let the injustice of the foundation go unpunished. This desire for justice would place them in the cross hairs of the foundation's assassin teams and any other resources they could muster. Joshua was not concerned; he was in control and would use any circumstance whether good or bad to work towards his final plan for the salvation of the human race.

He would use existing superhumans and other humans from the past, present and future. Alicia and Randy were the two parent figures in the family, and Cindy and Lee were the children. It was their growth that he would use as agents to bring superhumans together and fight in the Great War to come.

# Chapter Three

# Robbing Pastime

Romilly Street, London, September 15, 2007

W hisky dripped on the dark emerald countertop of the bar. Jason drank the Backstabber quickly and silently cheered by raising the empty shot glass in the air and then placing back on the counter. A group of people in Jason's party cheered out loud for him. The company cleared £9 million pounds and the celebration was well deserved for his employees.

His personal assistant and translator, Jonathan, patted Jason on the back. He smiled and signed to Jason, "you should take a deserved vacation Sir. It's good to see you happy like this."

Jason didn't return the smile, but he did nod as if contemplating the advice. Jason signed, "Thank you."

The night was young, but Jason left the party early, let Jonathan go for the night, and returned to his leased home. He went directly into the bathroom and showered. A short time afterwards he ended up in the study. The sound of Dvorak melodies echoed out of the room as Jason went over the final plans for a score in the Courtauld Institute of Art. He had stolen many paintings in the past, and made sure they were not worth more than forty million dollars, otherwise it would bring unnecessary attention, and would also be almost impossible to sell without leaving a trail to himself; however, this heist was a little different. He was not concerned about trying to steal and sell expensive items; he was focused on his techniques and abilities. He could infiltrate into almost any place and liked the challenge of defeating unique security systems.

He wanted to find out how far he could get before the alarm was given, so he planned to break into the art institute gallery and patrol the area over a week's period. The excitement of the situation was something he wanted to do, maybe trying to drown out the pain he felt for not doing what was right in the past. Or was it just the thrill of the hunt in particular the money? Jason was not sure what he wanted in life, he had a successful business, he didn't have a soul mate, but that was his choosing whether intentional or defensive, and he had no true friends, probably because he made it a point not to make friends. Every time he gave to charity or helped out someone in need, it brought peace to his heart, but only for a moment.

Life was funny and something in his being told him to keep his options and eyes open, and in time the meaning of life for him would be revealed.

Jason chose Monday for the first break in, simply because it was the first day of a normal work week. The London streets were busy and even more at night, but the gallery closed to the public at 6pm, and most of the employees left after 8pm. The lowest number of people in the gallery started at 10pm when it would be locked down by security after the maintenance and janitorial crews left for home. There were ten security guards, with two up to four constantly roaming specific areas of the museum, while the other areas were monitored by security sensors and cameras. Jason had reconnoitered the museum six months ago and also in the past four weeks as an art lover.

His business in London had him there for three more months, but this was part of the cover which made him less of a suspect in case the authorities somehow fingered him.

The night was cool with dense cloud cover at dinner time. Jason dressed like a normal guy going on a night out to a nightclub. He walked eight miles to his target where he skirted the river walkway and vanished into the shadows south of the museum.

It was 8pm and the south side of the museum was lit up with security lights, but this did not stop Jason from leaping a hundred meters into the air directly on top of the large building corner. His completely black outfit helped him blend in with the shadows outside, but the inside of the building was more exposed with abundant lighting and large open rooms.

The roof cameras and motion sensors where working perfectly for their intended use, but Jason was not the average thief and defied the sensors by being able to see the sensors and their infrared and ultraviolet emissions. He knew the exterior windows and doors would be monitored by both cameras and internal sensors, so his best hope was to go through the roof. He knew that the first infiltration was the key to future break ins, so he intentionally triggered an external door on the roof, which led to a machinery room for the right wing elevators. He entered the room and hid inside a duct way. A security guard and a maintenance worker arrived a few minutes later.

Both men did not see any signs of a break in and attributed the faulty door alarm to a power surge or temporary power outage. Jason had picked this museum because of the size of the ductwork which was inches large enough for him to maneuver inside. It didn't extend into all the areas of the museum, but more than half of the areas he needed to infiltrate without being seen were accessible through the duct work. Jason was ten feet inside the air shaft and could sense the men leaving the room before he heard them close the interior door. This was his chance, so he spent thirty minutes overriding the outside door with a bypass which allowed him to enter without alerting the computer system. The second stage was easier, which was to map out a route through the duck work, hallways, elevator shaft, and main gallery entry ways. He had to find the video junctions, and gain access to the camera feeds in order to create a circular feed of his own.

His sixth sense and specialized vision allowed him to see the areas that were covered by motion sensors, thermo cameras, and magnetic pressure sensors. The targeted three paintings he looked at were not all covered by guard patrols, which actually made it easy for him to spend an hour in front of each painting. The night was spent mostly taking notes of sensor readjustment frames, guard patrol times, and guard biographical backgrounds.

Jason left the museum before 7am on Tuesday morning. He spent the next six hours in his private office going through normal day emails and examining the layout for exit routes, alternate routes, and personnel backgrounds. The last two hours of the day he addressed company business and last minute emails.

The next day was less taxing, even though the guards changed their routes, the times remained consistent with a schedule of the week. He spent more time in front of the three targeted paintings, and had time to sketch out the paintings, frames, and surroundings of each painting. He never kept the sketches or diagrams he used and burned all evidence of his activities and targets on the last day prior to each job. He would decide by Saturday which painting he would take with him on Sunday.

The rest of the work week was uneventful, and he came to know the guards better and wondered if they would be punished severely for letting a painting come up missing. After some thought, he knew that the guards may get retrained, but in the end if anyone did lose a job, it would be because the person in charge had no understanding or appreciation for a master thief.

It was early Saturday morning when Jason approached his second nominee of a painting, but his sixth sense caught something in the next corridor. He could not tell if it was a guard who had randomly walked his route early or if there was someone else who was trespassing into his territory.

He had moved out of the air duct into the room a few minutes ago, but kept to the shadows on the far side of the corridor and waited to see if the person or thing would come out into his vision. He heard movement which seemed to be very far but yet close since the corridor was less than twenty meters long.

A very small object the size of a mosquito flew in the corridor and Jason could barely notice it except that it did not fly around like an insect, but hovered in the same location like a helicopter.

The small object increased in size to that of an uncommonly tall six foot female dressed in a dark blue and black flight suit outfit. She had goggles on, but Jason could tell that she had long hair by the bulge on her head which indicated it was bundled up in her cap like headgear.

She stood in front of the sculpture of King David, and walked up to it as if she was going to just grab it.

If she touched the sculpture and moved it, she would trigger an electronic sensor which was placed on each piece of art. Jason jumped out of his hiding place fifteen meters forward almost on top of the mystery woman.

The woman was startled and jumped backwards and sideways away from Jason. She shrunk almost instantly, but not small enough to fool Jason's senses. He put up his hands in front of him with palms open like if telling her to stop, but said nothing. The woman flew upward high and close to the ceiling. Jason followed her with his head and eyes. He motioned her with hand gestures to come down and stand in front of him. She flew away from him down the corridor, and stopped at the entrance to a spiral stairway.

Jason folded his arms and looked in her direction, but only for a moment, then he jumped back up to the air duct, entered it and made his way to the painting he liked the most out of the three nominees and decided to steal it now instead of waiting for Sunday night. He kept alert for the mosquito woman while he approached his target. As he exited the nearest air duct to the target, the alarm went off in the gallery and the painting he was about to steal was rapidly being covered by a metallic security screen. He assumed the cameras he had disabled were still disabled, but the security screen was seconds from the edge of his targeted painting.

Jason didn't have enough time to set a magnetic blocker on the frame of the painting so he tore off the frame from the wall and expertly cut out the painting from the rear. He dropped the frame next to the door of the Wolfson room and jumped towards the fire exit door opposite the painting as the security screens finished covering the intended walls. He made his way to the nearest air duct carrying with him a rolled up painting of, 'Portrait of a Woman.'

Jason was not completely sure if the camera setting was still actively repeating a loop, so he quickly made his way to the roof and retrieved his security cycling device. The exit door alarm rang once he stepped outside, but he ignored it as he leaped away from the museum into the darkness of the night. He leaped from building to building until he was fifteen miles away, then he headed into an alley where he instantly changed clothes. He walked down the alley and emerged on the corner of a coffee and bread shop. He bought a French bread and a few other items. He exited the shop and used the bread bag to hide the painting. He placed the bread on a bus stop seat, and continued walking towards his home which was three miles away.

## Chapter Four

# Love at First Sight

### London, United Kingdom

I t was a clear night sky, while Jason walked slowly and ate a donut. He felt his sixth sense again telling him, he was being watched. It sort of confused him, wondering why he noticed it now and not before. His home was two blocks away now, and he felt uncomfortable about going into his house without knowing who was spying on him. He went past his house and walked toward a nearby park. A small playground area was empty of people, but there were some people that would visit the park in the middle of the night after the bar scene or for a romantic chat with a boyfriend or girlfriend. It was Saturday night and someone would be there eventually, but that didn't matter to him. His sixth sense would tell him if it was the spy or a regular person who came from a bar or other location. He spent ten minutes on the swing with his painting lying across on his lap. He did not see, hear, or smell anyone, but his sixth sense told him otherwise. A person was nearby; otherwise he would not be feeling his inner sixth sense so intensely. He thought about the woman at the museum, but he would have sensed her presence no matter how small she got. He thought about other possibilities and it occurred to him that the person spying on him might be invisible. He had never met a superhuman who could become invisible, but he had heard that they existed. What were the chances of an invisible superhuman following him though? He thought some more and looked for things out of place or movement of things out of the ordinary. He also intently focused on his keen sixth sense which could indicate if the presence got closer or further away.

A few minutes passed and there was nothing, but in the distance he sensed a familiar presence. The woman from the museum was approaching. She was a good distance away, maybe four blocks away as she flew quickly behind him and stopped at the edge of the playground dirt. She was as small as a hummingbird and landed on the ground.

Jason turned his swing to face her, and signed, 'My name is Jason, who are you?'

The woman grew to her normal size, but was wearing a pleasant light colored cream reddish rustic dress this time. She was not wearing glasses or goggles, and Jason could see her beautiful blue eyes in the darkness of the park. Her long brown hair and arching eye brows elegantly matched her perfect lips and rounded cheeks. "You cannot talk?" She asked the obvious.

Jason signed again, 'You are a bright one. What is your name?'

The woman looked at him funny. "I don't know what you are saying, but it looks like you are introducing yourself, and you understand what I am saying. If I am right nod your head."

Jason smiled and nodded yes.

"I'm called Val. I followed you here after I saw you in the museum. It seems you have the same line of work as I do."

Jason slowly pulled out a pen and small note pad from his chest pocket. He wrote, 'My name is Jason. You triggered the alarm, so it seems we do not have the same line of work.' He held it out for her to take, and stayed seated in the swing.

Valerie was a little hesitant to grab the note, but she stepped forward, took it, and read it as she stepped two steps backwards. "Hmm, well you caused me to rush it."

Jason swung around and stood up, then turned back around facing her. His senses were on full alert and he noticed a slight movement in the dirt about six feet to his left. It was a partial footprint, and he now knew that the invisible spy was probably working for, or with Val. She had not been following him, and it was this spy who told her where he was. He wrote in his pad once again and tore out one page. 'Why were you following me?'

Valerie took the note with caution and read it. "I want to offer you a job."

Jason wrote again, but he kept the page on the pad and held it up so she could read it. 'Who is your friend?'

Valerie had to step closer to read the writing. Once Jason

was sure she had read it, he moved forward with lightning speed and grabbed her, twisting her so he was grabbing her from behind. He grabbed Valerie with great strength around the neck with one hand. Valerie was completely taken by surprise, but she did not shrink instantly to try to get away.

Jason sensed a foot impression move in his direction, and he leaped back away from it about ten feet taking Valerie with him, "Tell him to stop." Jason spoke breaking his rule for the first time in almost two decades.

Valerie did not say anything, but she held up her hand motioning the invisible spy to stop where he was.

"I can break your neck before you can shrink. Now tell me who you really are?"

"So, Jason speaks." Valerie replied.

"Tell him or her to show himself." Jason commanded with a tighter grip on her neck, but noticed that her body was denser and a lot stronger than any human he knew; she could probably be hung on a noose and nothing would happen.

"It's okay Sia." Valerie said without any major discomfort from the grip on her neck which would have normally been choking an average person into desperation for air.

A man appeared out of thin air ten feet from them. Jason instantly sensed the man's distinct odor being downwind now that he was not cloaked with invisibility. His Asian complexion revealed Japanese linage, but his clothing was that of a well dressed English businessman. He stood to be about six feet and was very muscular, but yet very slim.

"Who are you guys?"

"We can talk better without your hand on my neck." Valerie said.

Jason released his hold on Valerie and stepped backwards, then went to the painting which had dropped on the ground.

Kyle walked next to Valerie as Jason picked up the painting. "How did you know I was here?" Kyle asked in perfect English.

"The same way I knew Val was in the museum, and the same way I knew she did not follow me here. It is because of you that I came to the park. I needed to see who you were." Jason explained.

"I'm Valerie, and this is Kyle, also known as Sia." Valerie made the late introduction.

"I'm Jason Norton." Jason said, knowing that telling them a lie would not be good, since they had already seen his face and would be able to link it to his current identity as Jason. "But you still haven't told me who you are?"

Valerie understood his question, "We are thieves like you. We have been in a thieves' guild for about a year."

"So you work for someone else?" Jason asked.

Valerie and Kyle stayed silent for a moment. "Well we can do what we want." Kyle said.

"Really, so who decided to steal King David?"

"I decided." Valerie said.

"Did you know that you will not be able to fence it or sell it yourself even with guild connections." Jason asked.

"You underestimate our connections and resources." Valerie said.

"We can steal almost anything." Kyle proudly said.

"Stealing is not the only thing you have to know; being able to sell things is just as important." Jason said as he sat back down on one of the three swings.

"Really, so where do you plan on selling that painting of yours?" Kyle asked, knowing it was a very hot painting.

"I'm not, it will be returned in a week or two."

Valerie and Kyle looked at Jason amused, "Well, we're not here to swap ideas, we are here to ask you to join us?" Valerie asked.

"Why me, it seems you two have no problems doing your thing, and I am doing very well by myself."

"We don't normally recruit people, but you have something we want and who knows what we can achieve together?"

Jason thought for a moment, "I will listen to what you have to say, but on one condition."

"What is that?" Valerie asked.

"I have not talked for many years, and my survival sometimes depends on me being mute. I don't know you that well, and I'm not a very good judge of character, but I do know that if you guys betray me I will kill you." Jason explained with a deadly serious demeanor.

Valerie looked at him not knowing if she should not worry or if he was going to be a problem for the group. "So, you're telling me that I have to learn sign language?"

Kyle looked at both of them. "Well Diana will not like this."

Jason looked at Kyle, then Valerie.

"Diana is the third person in our group. I was going to tell you about her." Valerie explained.

"I see, and where is she now?" Jason asked.

"She is probably back home with the statue." Kyle said.

"Well, yes, everyone will have to learn sign language, it is my one condition, and besides, it helps in people under estimating me thinking I can't speak."

"I don't think your past can be that bad, but time will tell. In the meantime, let's go somewhere better suited for talking." Valerie suggested.

"Follow me" Jason walked them to his house.

They arrived at the house and the three sat down in the living room. They talked for an hour before calling Diana to join them. Jason revealed a few things about his past, in particular, that he used to be a terrorist, but the group did not mind too much with their own shady histories. Diana had murdered people in her past, Kyle and Valerie also had killed people in their misguided fashions, but none of them out rightly killed innocent people like Jason. They concluded that it would be in the best interest of the group and Jason to treat Jason as a mute, but he would have to give up his life and start a new one as someone else who had no connections to any company, family, or friends.

Jason was not used to following orders, especially after the death of his fiancé, but he would give this group a chance. The more he saw Valerie's face and heard her sweet voice, the more he wanted to be closer to her. She seemed more refined than most women he had met. Her penetrating blue eyes and elegant poise demonstrated an upper class upbringing, and this intrigued him because all the thieves he knew started from the bottom of the classes.

The group stayed in Jason's home for several days and waited for the income of the statue to be secured. To Jason's surprise, the connections which this group had been extremely efficient, which made him worry. Their boss was very powerful and connected, and he knew that placing himself vulnerable to this person may leave room for betrayal if he or the group did not do what was directed or expected.

In the meantime, he enjoyed everyone's company, especially Valerie's. Diana was extremely smart, but had her sadistic flaws, and Kyle was a bit egotistical, but Mathew had his moments as well, of which Valerie was very curious about. They had many things in common, to include pastimes like taking long walks and seeing the country side. It was very peaceful for him, and it seemed to do the same thing for her.

His new identity would be Fredrick Malleson, an art insurance consultant and entrepreneur. Jason's company would be placed in good hands, and his faked death would separate him from his past once again. His identity within the group was Mathew, no last name, just Mat or Mathew.

However, it seemed to Mathew, that the identities they had were not enough, and he made his first suggestion to the group, which was to use cover names in public. Kyle did not like the idea until Mathew suggested they use nicknames after a known television show. Diana liked the idea from the start and chose Nyota. Kyle quickly jumped in and chose Khan, while Mathew chose James, and Valerie, Janice. It was not a good way of having a cover, but to the normal public, their names would blend in and they would have some fun out of it like actors in a movie or play.

It took a few weeks before Mathew was officially Fredrick, and they were given another assignment in the months to come. Mathew was a born leader and his senses made him best suited for command and control. It wasn't long before Kyle and both women elected Mathew to be leader of the nameless group in a guild which apparently didn't exist. Each group member did have a code name (Hummel, Hawk, Sia, and Venom), which their employer insisted on, but they rarely used their respective code names and stuck to their nicknames or group names. In the end, each member had a myriad of names which would be used at different times and circumstances. The names were just a formality and their secret identities would not be compromised by them or their employer who had them going to the United States in the coming years to perform the heist of the century.

As months passed, Mathew and Valerie could not help

but fall deeply in love with each other. Their wedding was a simple indoor event with a priest, public notary as a witness, and judge all provided by their employer, Sir David Lanhurst. The honeymoon was a month long in Switzerland, along with a trip to Alyssa's burial site in Nepal. To Mathew it was a way of letting go of the past and embracing the future with Valerie. For Valerie, it was necessary psychological therapy and healing for them both as they set off together as husband and wife.

## Chapter Five

# Christmas Get Together

### 1601 Arapahoe Street, Denver, Colorado, December 19, 2007

Randy tapped on the frost covered window. His finger nails caused loud sharp sounds of metal on tempered glass to spread across the large open loft.

The covers of the bed behind him moved to one side as Alicia's head came into view. "What's wrong Baby?"

Randy turned to face her and smiled, "It's almost Christmas."

Alicia tiredly looked at the LED clock on the nightstand. "No, it's almost three AM, come back to bed." She closed her eyes and laid her head back on her plush pillow.

Randy came up to the side of the bed, placed one knee on the bed and dragged the other leg. He avidly kissed her awake and messaged her entire body. They had passionate sex before sleeping the rest of the morning.

Their slumber was interrupted by the sound of the television alarm. The morning local 4 news started their day, along with some more foreplay and sweet loving.

They both shared in making a late breakfast and ate in bed watching the Hallmark channel special presentations. The day had started out wonderful in Alicia's eyes, but Randy was feeling disturbed, but dared not tell her. She would insist on making him talk about what was making him worry or angry.

It had been over three years since they had been freed from the Yemen complex, but his heart was still enslaved to revenge. Alicia didn't speak of revenge for two years now, but he knew that she was also troubled by their inaction. Late last night while Alicia slept, Randy saw a report of a bus bomb which had the foundations fingerprints, which is why he could not sleep for several hours.

Christmas time seemed to bring up the past in a flood of emotions, with the desire to punish the foundation, but also a message to love and forgive others. They had been freed right before Christmas and it was a time to celebrate, but also reminded them of the foundation. Joshua would talk to them every now and then, and each time he would tell him and Alicia how much they were loved. It kept them at peace, but the more they investigated or saw that the foundation was not changing their evil ways, the more they wanted to change it for them.

It was mid day when they bathed together and prepared to go grocery shopping for the big celebration to come. Lee and Cindy were scheduled to visit them in a few days, and they were going to make this Christmas and New Years as happy as it could be for the entire family.

The supermarket was very crowded that Wednesday, and many sales were advertised. They were able to find all of the items on their list, plus some pleasant extras in the form of fresh fruits to make fruit shakes. They loved to eat well and made it a point to know how to cook. The rest of the day was spent in their warm loft with the smell of freshly baked apple pie and cinnamon bread. They lay together lazily watching movies and listening to holiday music.

Lee called them late evening to verify his arrival to the city from Los Angeles by the afternoon on the next day. Cindy had not contacted them in a few months, but that was not unusual for her. She was the youngest and most mischievous as she regularly stole money and information from the mafia underground in order to supplement her job as a computer consultant. She would surely turn up in a day or two, and was well capable of protecting herself, but even then Alicia worried about her welfare every new season.

Alicia and Randy had their own website dating business called True Love Connect, which generated a constant income, but it was Alicia's way of trying to find Cindy and Lee a good person in their lives. It didn't work out as she planned, because they both hated looking for someone online or through other venues, but many people did like it and so the business blossomed.

That night, Randy couldn't hold it in and told Alicia about the bus bomb killing thirty-four people, which brought about a long conversation about their future. The next morning came and both of them cleaned the loft, and adjacent lofts which they owned as well to include specially constructed connecting doors between the lofts. The complex of lofts was way too big for them alone, but company was coming and they liked to be able to accommodate their two visiting family members.

The Denver International Airport was extremely busy with packed traffic, but they made it there just in time to see Lee come out of the passageway from the gate entrance. Lee had tinted his hair a little lighter shade of brown, still had a spiky style cut on top, and had grown it out to slightly cover his ears but was trimmed neatly from the back of the neck. He carried a dark gray backpack and an mp3 player. His blue eyes were covered by dark sunglasses.

"Bradley!" Alicia quickly ran up to Lee and gave him a big hug. "Merry Christmas!"

Randy casually walked up and followed suit. "How was the flight?"

"It was slow, but it's great now." Lee grinned.

Lee looked at Randy's wedding ring. "When did that happen, who for that matter?" Then he looked at Alicia's ring and connected the dots. "How long?"

"It's been a week." Alicia smiled, both of them holding each other by the waist.

"Why didn't you two tell me earlier?"

"We didn't want you and Sam to stay away or hurry here, so we thought we would surprise you." Randy said while Alicia continued to smile.

"Yes, it's a good surprise." They walked to the baggage pickup area. Lee was happy to see Randy and Alicia finally together. The couple was instantly attracted to each other the day they left the Yimen complex, and the marriage was well over due. Lee saw happiness inside of them and knew it was firmly founded on their love for each other. His last three years was jumping from city to city, making friends here and there, but he could never connect to any woman for a long lasting relationship. Maybe because he was a superhuman, always looking to get the bad guys, and simply didn't want to settle down. He had jumped from job to job in law enforcement, which gave him a very big ego boost. His military and law enforcement expertise allowed him to get temporary jobs in police departments across the country. It was temporary because he made it that way, with Joshua's help of course. This month was one of the off months, with his affiliation with the LAPD terminating a few weeks ago. He was now plain Bradley Williams, university student, on vacation from Pasadena, California.

The trio retrieved a large suitcase from the baggage carousel and they conversed about Lee's adventures all the way home.

Lee quickly settled into his exclusive small loft, but went next door and spent the rest of the time conversing and watching television while Randy and Alicia cooked supper. They did not mind it especially since Lee was their guest. No sooner had the last clean plate rested on the dinner table when the doorbell rang.

Randy cheerfully answered the door, knowing there was a very high probability it was Cindy. Yes, it was Cindy in a very elegant black dress covered by a maroon cashmere coat and hat to match. Cindy's once girlish body and face was now the envy of many swimsuit models. Her very long sandy blond hair draped over the front of her shoulders, and dark brown leather boots displayed a fashion statement she was very happy to show off.

"Wow! You look wonderful!" Randy said as he hugged his little sister.

"Why, thank you Randy?" Cindy smiled.

A scream came from the kitchen area and Alicia ran across from the corner of the trapezoid shaped loft to greet Cindy. "Cindy! Don't you know how to use the phone? Why didn't you call?"

Cindy entered the loft, hugged Alicia and then Lee. "You know me. I wanted to make sure I made it for dinner. If I had called you then you would have slowed or sped up serving dinner."

"How is it that you got here at the exact time dinner was ready? I mean you did that last year. Is there something you know that we don't." Lee asked.

Cindy looked a little confused. "No, I don't think so. Joshua told me when to be here."

"Really?" Randy said.

"Is there something Joshua wanted us to do or know?" Alicia asked.

"I don't know, why?" Cindy said still confused.

"Well what my lovely wife is trying to say is why would Joshua bother to tell you dinner times unless it had something to do with something of great importance?" Randy explained.

Cindy smiled. "Joshua told me about you two love birds getting married, and dinner, and Lee being here too."

"But, why did he tell you all those things?" Lee asked.

Cindy thought about it for a second. "I asked him."

Lee smiled. "Huh, I guess I should have asked for a winning lotto."

"Hmm, yeah I guess we should talk to Joshua more." Alicia said, knowing that Randy was also thinking the same thing. Their lives were busy with each other and talking to Joshua on a daily or weekly basis was something they stopped doing a few years ago.

Lee talked to Joshua, but more on a business sense dealing with everything at work, things to help him in improving his abilities or in a time of crisis. It seemed that Cindy was the one who talked to Joshua about everything personal and business related all the time.

The women went to the kitchen, while the men finished preparing the table with glasses filled with French burgundy wine, candles, and soft holiday background music. They enjoyed their savory prime rib beef roast dinner along with stories old and new about each other. Laughter and joy filled the loft for many hours into the night.

The next day involved shopping and visiting the Denver attractions. The group enjoyed several days of relaxation and entertainment. However, Lee noticed that Randy and Alicia had been keeping something inside, which kept them from fully enjoying the moment. He left it alone, hoping they would relieve what they were fighting against.

It was on Christmas Eve dinner when Lee broke the question at the table.

"What is bothering you two? What are you not telling us?" Lee asked out of nowhere as they talked about the 1946 movie 'It's a Wonderful Life'.

Everyone was taken aback, but Alicia was the first to get serious. "Tell them Baby."

Cindy and Lee were silent.

"We were going to wait until after New Years." Randy paused while looking back and forth between Lee and Cindy. "There was a bomb on a bus the day before you two arrived. It was a foundation assassin team. They killed over twenty women and children in the process. Alicia and I have a plan to put an end to the killing, by killing them all."

"But, we can't do it alone'" Alicia added.

"Joshua told us to let them destroy themselves." Lee replied.

"And how many more good people need to die before they destroy themselves?" Randy countered.

"Not one more, I am with you guys." Cindy stated.

Lee looked at Cindy surprised. He thought that she would be the most passive about all this, but that may have been three years ago, not now that she was a young woman who was wiser and more mature. "Do you have any idea of how many people we are talking about?"

"About seventy people." Randy said.

"There are a whole lot more people in the foundation then that?" Lee said.

"Yes, but there are seventy-three key personnel, and without them the foundation will crumble for good."

"You are forgetting the people that will be guarding them."

"No, not really, there are only four people with body guards, and if we kill all eighty or so people in a short period of time, there won't be heavy security. I mean we have the element of surprise."

"So if I say no, then the surprise won't happen, right?" Lee asked.

Randy sighed, "Yeah, I guess that's right."

Lee looked at the three in deep thought, then at the golden brown stuffed turkey in front of him. "Let's finish this turkey, and then you can tell me how many people I need to kill."

Cindy grabbed Lee's wrist and smiled.

"What? I can't let you guys go in there without me. And besides, I'm the only one that can shoot straight."

"Yes, we know." Randy grinned.

"A toast to us, may we have more Christmases together!" Alicia said.

"Cheers! Merry Christmas! To Santa!" They toasted, laughed, and enjoyed the rest of the night going over the plan and Christmas movies. At midnight, they opened their presents and relaxed the rest of the morning.

Randy and Alicia were very meticulous with their research and scenarios. Lee was very impressed with the synchronization of the ambitious plan. They would each have to split up and kill specific targets at specific times of the day. It was a logistical nightmare which Randy and Alicia pulled off expertly.

The highlight of their plan was to kill fifty-four foundation members in one blow at an executive dinner scheduled for March. In addition, they would kill seven people on a yacht scheduled to be at sea on the same day. The remaining twelve people would have to be killed individually.

It was critical that the twelve individuals and yacht people were quietly killed first, leaving the ballroom last.

The physical challenge was the distance between targets, which meant that Lee would have to take care of six individuals over a five state area since he was the fastest flyer. Cindy would take care of the yacht. Randy and Alicia would have to split three people a piece, and then attack the Cardigan International building ballroom. Lee would have just enough time to make it to the building should they need backup.

They knew that collateral damage might claim innocent lives. The caterers and innocent spouses were the ones they would have to worry about in the ballroom since no children were allowed to participate, otherwise everything should go smoothly.

Before New Year's Day, Joshua spoke to them in their dreams telling them that there were consequences which they would have to accept should they follow through with their plan. As usual, Joshua would only advise and guide them; if they elected not to follow his counsel; it was their wise or unwise choice.

They talked about it and would all see it through; whatever consequences, it was a matter of not allowing the foundation to continue to kill or harm innocent people and families because of their inaction.

# Chapter Six

# Phase I

## Barnett Bank, Dallas Texas, May 6, 2011

The clear night cold air vibrated the tall skyscraper's windowed structure. The street below was abandoned with scraps of trash debris moving across the pavement from the city's windy currents. Kyle stood on the building's ledge surveying the street and city below as a police cruiser made its routine patrol rounds. He was completely invisible to the world and was totally content standing on the ledge as his associates initiated Phase I of the ultimate robbery of all time.

The skyscraper's large bank lobby floor stood motionless as stationary wide angle cameras scanned the area from corner to corner. The sixth camera at the left corner of the lobby went black as an aluminum cover was placed over the optics. A ghostly hand retracted into the ceiling, and then one by one the remaining eight cameras and four motion detectors were neutralized. The vault interior camera revealed an empty chamber of static safe deposit boxes and money shelves. In less than a few minutes this last camera fell to the same fate as the ones in the lobby.

A ghostly figure of a woman phased out of the vault ceiling and dropped to the floor. She walked up to the vault's motion detector and placed a prism like device against it. A green light appeared in the center of the prism then faded away. Diana materialized into a solid state and drew out a piece of paper from her pocket. Her long curly red hair bounced slightly as she walked up to the safe deposit boxes examining the labels, and one by one opened the pre-designated containers.

Valerie being the size of an ant gracefully flew out of Diana's pocket and to the center of the vault floor. In an instant, she grew into a full sized woman wearing a brown outfit with black stripes on each side of her body running from her ankles to the top of her shoulders. She wore large dark ski goggles and a small backpack filled with a metallic rectangular device and netting. She took out a net like blanket from her pack and placed it on the floor.

Diana tossed bundles of money, certificates, safe deposit boxes and jewelry to the center of the room while Valerie arranged the loot on top of the net. In a matter of minutes, the pile of riches had been stacked six feet tall and nine feet in diameter. Diana closed and secured all of the safe deposit boxes as Valerie tied and wrapped the pile of money and jewelry with the loose ends of the net at the apex of the stack.

Valerie jumped on top of the stack and sat there for just a moment as the entire bundle of money and jewelry shrunk along with her into the size of walnut.

Diana reached inside her pocket and placed a four inch tall stainless steel statue of a hawk on the vault floor. She proceeded to casually pick up her co-worker, placed her and the loot inside her left breast pocket and flew up phasing through the vault ceiling. Several minutes elapsed with all of the bank cameras coming back to life, except for the entrance door monitors.

A smelly raggedy bum laid in an alleyway across from the bank entrance as Diana phased through the inner metal security curtain and double glass doors. Diana's costume turned into a long black overcoat as she turned to face the bank entrance doors. She stuck her ghost like hand inside of the doors triggering the silent alarm. Diana smiled as she twirled around and tighten the waist cords around her slim figure. She casually walked down the street a few blocks and turned the corner disappearing into the night.

The bum laid there witnessing the woman leave the scene with curiosity. He observed the woman's face in the dim street lights then covered himself tighter with a half torn blanket as semi-cold air gushed between the buildings. Five minutes passed by when he noticed blue and red lights approaching the bank. The man stood up as the lights were turned off and police cars quietly pulled in front of the bank. He walked back into the alley, away from the crime scene only to melt into the shadows. His ragged clothes transformed into a comfortable leather jacket and black cotton slacks. Matthew walked to the other side of the alley and got into a dark green 1994 Thunderbird. The police scanner automatically turned on as he keyed the ignition and drove off to meet his partners in crime who awaited his final report.

## West Virginia, May 14, 2011

Diana casually laid on a lounge chair by the pool. The remains of small ice cubes swirled around the filled glass of lemonade. She idly held the end of the straw completely bored to death. Her red long hair complemented her dark red lip stick. Her green eyes stared into a void of space, even though the majestically decorated customized pool and surrounding European style garden encircled her with beauty. The 17$^{th}$ century mansion behind her portrayed a wealthy life style which most people could only dream of having their entire lives, but it seemed so plain to her. It had been a week since she strolled through the city streets of Dallas. The bank job pulled in an extra $350,000 dollars into her already enormous bank accounts.

Her mind was elsewhere as Kyle swam laps across the thirty meter pool. He finished his hundredth lap and jumped out of the water in front of Diana. "Hey gorgeous, what are you thinking about?"

Diana looked across the pool. "I'm bored. Hey, why don't we go out to the range and spar a little?"

Kyle thought about the challenge for a second. "I don't think so. I've had enough pain for today."

Diana looked at Kyle in contempt. "You're such a baby. Sometimes I wonder why you're in the group." She said trying to make Kyle angry.

"That won't work D. You cheated last time and nearly killed me."

Diana smiled as she recalled scratching Kyle's arm and injecting venom into his blood stream. "I promise I won't do that again." She innocently smiled and blinked her sexy eye lashes.

"When we do, I won't hold back; but not today." Kyle declined.

Diana smugly smirked at Kyle, "You're such a baby."

"Whatever." Kyle nodded and jumped across the pool performing acrobatic stunts in the air gracefully landing on the other side with very little effort.

Valerie and Matthew walked down the pool walkway in front of Kyle. "So, what's up Mat?" Kyle asked knowing they had a job lined up.

Matthew signed very quickly with his hands. Kyle was still not fluent in sign language and looked at Valerie a little confused. "Knots?"

"He said we're going shopping for gold at Ft. Knox." Valerie translated.

Kyle's smiled and nodded with satisfaction, "Nice."

"Okay, it's going to take some extra planning time in order for us to stay on schedule."

Diana approached standing and sliding a few inches above the water across the pool overhearing the conversation. "So how much gold are we taking?"

Valerie looked at Kyle and Diana. "An eighteen wheeler full."

Diana looked at Mat and Valerie with amusement. "You can't shrink that much." Diana said, stating the obvious knowing Valerie's limitations.

"Not yet." Valerie smiled.

Mat signed again. 'That's why we're preparing and not just running in there like amateurs.'

"What are we waiting for then, let's go." Kyle joyfully said leading the way into the mansion.

"Wait! There is another thing." Valeria interrupted.

"David wants to meet us after the next heist."

Kyle and Diana looked inquisitive. "Why would he want to meet us?" Diana asked.

"I don't know, but Mathew never trusted him from the beginning so if any of you have any objections, he recommends we have a retirement strategy." Valerie explained.

"I don't trust many people, but he pays all the bills and we don't have to worry about working with idiots. So, what are we talking about exactly." Kyle commented.

"I never cared too much for his trust, but do you think we should bite the hand that feeds us good jobs?" Diana asked.

'We have been together for over a year and yes he has given us good jobs, but I feel that the last job is not right and will be nothing but trouble for us.' Mathew signed.

"We need to find out what he is up to. Ever since Evergreen showed up in Florida, I know that something is being covered up by David." Valerie stated.

"You never mentioned she was there." Kyle said annoyed.

"We didn't tell you because Creator was patrolling the area and saw Mat and Val. Creator ended up going after the truck but Evergreen got rid of the evidence." Diana explained.

Kyle thought about the events several months ago in Miami. They had scouted out a factory and nearby warehouse with stolen space equipment. Creator, the leader of the Eternal Champions - a superhero group stationed in Ft. Lauderdale, must have been the trigger to abort the mission. The truck which left the warehouse and blew up in a huge ball of fire was also probably the stolen goods David didn't want other people to have. Evergreen was a superhuman and special operative for David Lanhurst. She was a flying natural disaster with powers to create and control infrared wavelengths to unheard of extremes, even by superhuman standards. In all essence, she was David's only and most effective cleaner.

"And you couldn't tell me sooner?" Kyle asked still annoyed that he was left out of the loop.

'Because we didn't want you to go off on your own and spy on Creator.' Mathew signed.

"What, you don't think I'm good enough?"

"They have telepaths and would have found you out." Diana bluntly stated.

'When Creator was tracking us I could sense I was being mentally scanned. If it wasn't for the fact that we followed our escape routes, and Creator went after the truck, it would have been much harder to have eluded him and his team.' Mathew commented.

"So what are we going to do about Sir Lancelot?" Kyle got back to the root subject.

"After this gold heist, I will see what I can find out about Evergreen. Kyle you will do some heavy research on David. Mat and D will work out our options." Valerie stated Mat's specific instructions.

'Sound good to you guys?' Mathew asked.

"Sounds like a plan." Diana replied.

Several hours later, the backup generator activated instantly after the entire power grid failed to channel electricity into the outlining sectors of the city. Valerie continued to work on her computer screen ignoring the power outage as the backup power supply system automatically activated long enough for the mansion's generators to kick in.

Kyle and Diana also continued to draw up plans of attack looking at schematics of the Fort Knox treasury.

Matthew noticed the ceiling light flicker long after the generators activated, and instinctively scanned the area for any approaching danger. He sensed no danger, but something was out of place. He stopped working and turned on the television. He clicked the remote scanning the channels and noticed the local channels weren't working. He flipped to CNN and didn't have to wait long before reports of a killer computer virus hit the headlines. He clapped his hands out of habit, drawing the team's attention instead of yelling. The team watched the report get interrupted by static as the virus hit the satellite relay station.

Matthew quickly looked at Valerie making a motion to the laptop.

Valerie jumped and flew towards the laptop with incredible speed, unplugging the LAN cable. She attempted to unlock the blank screen, but it was too late. Both hard drives were formatted with garbage text, and the network hub was completely at the mercy of the virus.

"Dammit! We lost everything." Valerie cursed at herself for not saving the new changes. Her back up files were a few hours old, with very little information on their new hit.

"What do we do now?" Kyle asked.

'We stick to the plan and start over. I will see if we can get an extra week to execute the hit.' Matthew signed.

"Well I guess this wasn't a boring day after all." Diana smiled.

"What about just using the leader's recon to get the info we need, and use this virus to help mask our movements?" Kyle asked.

Mathew looked at Valerie and nodded approval. "Okay I guess I can sketch out the areas and things."

'You see it helps out when you appreciate good art' Mathew smiled.

Valerie smiled back. "I guess those drawing lessons will be put to good use."

"In the meantime, do you think the reservation was erased with this virus thing?" Valerie asked.

"Hmmm, well we should go early, cuz I'm not going to sleep at a Motel 6." Kyle stated.

"Since when do we ever stay in motels?" Diana asked.

Kyle stared into space and smiled. "Yea, you're right."

'I'm pretty sure the airports have been shut down, so let's pack up for a road trip.

"Too bad we can't stay here longer." Valerie sighed.

Diana looked at her friend. "Don't tell me you're going soft with being married and all?"

"It's because of Mat that I haven't retired." Valerie countered.

"You're too young to retire."

"That's what he said." Valerie said.

'No, I said retirement is too young for us.' Mat corrected.

"Well that's true, it's not like you need the money or the time. We have that every day." Diana added.

"I will know when it's time to stop stealing things." Valerie said.

"Hopefully, not when we get caught." Kyle joked.

"Hush, that's not in our vocabulary." Diana said.

"I have looked a long time for what I wanted in life, and I found it in my wife and my friends." Mathew verbally said.

It was a break in protocol for Mathew to speak, but they appreciated the gesture as it was something extremely important for him to convey. Mathew spoke with Valerie quietly in bed most of the time; otherwise his cover was maintained quite effectively no matter the situation. In effect, Mathew was waiting for the last person who knew him to die of old age, before he would consider speaking on a regular basis. His brother passed away several years ago, and maybe he was being paranoid, but he knew him acting as a mute may save people's lives one day. The survival of the group and the guild relied on being invisible to the world, something he and those around him were very good at doing.

'But keep your ears and eyes open to what this virus is doing. It might get in our way, so we will need to do things without relying on our tech stuff too much.' Mathew instructed.

"Okay let's pack up lite then." Valerie added and went upstairs.

# Chapter Seven

# The Plan

### Madison Street, Plymouth, North Carolina, March 17, 2010

L ee was the first to execute their synchronized assassinations. It was a clear night sky as he silently landed on the rooftop of the Whitely house. He was covered by a flat black armored suit extending no more than an inch or two from his skin. It was opaque and made him look like a robotic computer generated image of a male silhouette of a suited space soldier. There were no markings and no facial features were visible on a helmet type covering resembling a riot control blast shield. A small flat backpack and state of the art precision looking rifle were the only two distinct external pieces of equipment. Lee could see inside the master bedroom through the roof tiles and ceiling with his specialized optics. Mr. Whitely watched television as his wife slept next to him. "In position." Lee said into his helmet microphone.

"Got you, ready here." Alicia replied.

"Okay everything is a go." Randy added.

"On board." Cindy replied and shut off her radio.

Lee flew down through the roof and into the master bedroom. There was no loud crash or major breaking of the structure as Lee expertly used his rifle's laser setting to cut a hole through the tiles, beams, insulation, and drywall like a knife through butter. The noise from the debris of a section of ceiling hitting the master bedroom floor woke up Mrs. Whitely. Before anyone could scream or speak, the couple felt a very blunt force as the concessional effects of Lee's rifle knocked them unconscious. Lee quickly made sure the main bedroom door was locked and then took an electrical wire from the adjacent lamp and hog tied Mrs. Whitely. He gagged and blind folded her with clothes from the walk-in closet. He then grabbed Mr. Whitely by the head and twisted it until he was dead. He took the cell phones in plain view, broke them, and yanked out the hard line phone connection. His last action was to turn off the television and unlock the bedroom door. It took less than two minutes before Lee was off to his next target.

### West Greenfield Ave, Milwaukee, Wisconsin

Randy entered an open apartment window with great ease. Ms. Devin was on her laptop as Randy came up behind her and hit her on the back of her head crushing her skull with his fist. The impact drove her face into the computer screen and flatten it out as blood splattered all over. Her body rested lifeless on the table and computer while he went to the kitchen and washed away the blood from his hand.

Randy did not bother to unplug the computer, as he left the same way he came in knowing there was no one else in the apartment.

### Burton Street SE, Grand Rapids, Michigan

Alicia checked her electronic tracker to confirm the vehicle she was following. She smelled and heard Mr. Wall's distinctive identifiers and flew down directly over the Dodge Viper. He was alone, but the car was in motion and if she waited for him to stop at a red light or turn there would be witnesses. She waited for a clearing of traffic and she swopped down and touched the top of the front windshield. The glass instantly shattered and Mr. Wall frantically swerved off the street into a car wash vacuum cleaner. The car came to a sudden stop as the concrete base and poles overpowered the car frame. Mr. Wall was pinned between the deployed airbag and the seat as Alicia touched his head and shattered his skull into hundreds of pieces. The vibrations from her touch and bone fragments in his brain killed him instantly.

Alicia did not look around but simply flew straight up into the night sky towards her second target.

### Off the coast of Ocean City, Maryland

Cindy flew over her target completely invisible to the world; easily defeating the Trinity yacht's radar. She spread out the molecules in her body and floated inside the yacht on the forward lower deck. She walked throughout the vessel confirming all seven targets. They were all presently scattered about, but there were three yacht workers and two guests not on the target list. Blowing up the yacht was out of the question, but she expected this so she started with the most secluded people and one by one, she placed a plate she picked up from the kitchen inside the neck of each victim separating their head from their body for a split second. She then grabbed the victim and spread out their molecules. She and the dead victim floated downward through the hull into the ocean. She released the body and flew back up into the yacht. The last two victims took more time, because she had to wait for one of the guest and worker to look away as she turned the victim invisible upon making deliberate contact with him. In less than ten minutes, all seven targets were in or floating on the dark Atlantic Ocean. There was a possibility the workers would search for the missing people and find remains near the vessel with their spotlights, but word would not get out until late that night or morning about the deaths, to the public or to the president of the Cardigan foundation at the dinner event.

Cindy did not like her handiwork but she was not ashamed of killing evil people who would not think twice about ordering or agreeing to her own death. She flew towards Chicago as fast as her powers allowed her.

### Billings, Montana

Lee approached the farm estate of his last target, Mr. Stiles. Stiles was retired, but his name was on the list because of his past reputation and knowledge of them. Lee could see four people on the farm; two young adults, one child, and Mr. Stiles. Lee knew him from the Yimen complex, but things did not add up.

Mr. Stiles was in his study listening to Mozart, but he had a glass of wine prepared for a guest.

'Talk to him. He is on your side' Joshua told Lee as if he were inside of his head.

Lee was going to fly into the study and shoot him, but stopped next to the sliding glass door. Lee slid open the unlocked door. Mr. Jonah Stiles turned to face Lee standing outside the door. "He told me you were coming, come in, sit." Stiles welcomed him.

Lee could see all the weapons in the house with his active en-ray vision and knew this was not a trap. Stile's personal hand gun was locked away by his bed, and his collection of unloaded rifles were in the weapon racks.

"Do they know I'm here?" Lee asked, walked inside but didn't sit in the sofa chair provided.

Stiles looked in the direction of his daughter, son-in-law, and grandchild even though they were on the other side of the house, "No, they are living a normal life, as we all should have done many years ago."

"You know why I am here?"

"I knew three years ago before Joshua gave his ultimatum that everyone involved with the foundation would be killed. I was so stupid a decade ago, but somehow I didn't see the prison I created for myself. Three years ago, I tried telling them to change, but they wouldn't listen."

"What ultimatum?" Lee asked, interested in what Joshua

had told Stiles three years ago.

"Joshua told the board members to change the way they did business, or he would kill them all. I didn't think he would use other people to accomplish his word."

"He didn't. We decided on this on our own." Lee explained.

"I'm only fifty-two years old, but I feel like a very old man. I don't know why Joshua let us have this discussion, but if you're not going to kill me now, can you at least sit and have a drink with me?"

Lee hesitated for a moment but sat down on the sofa chair. His helmet disappeared revealing his head. The rest of his energy body armor was intact, and light as a feather on the sofa. His rifle was absorbed by the armor and freed up his right hand. His optical sensors told him the wine was safe to drink. He picked up the glass of wine and toasted silently.

Stiles sat in his sofa chair in front of Lee and sipped his glass of wine. "I knew Joshua would not have allowed innocent people to die in the complex. It is good to know that I was right."

"What do you know of the foundation?"

"Well if you came for me, you must also know that you would have to kill over fifty people or more for the foundation to go under."

"We know, over half should be dead by now."

"I need to tell you that since Joshua's ultimatum, they acquired two special psychics. They thought that if they could see

Joshua coming they could fight him. They are no match for Joshua, but they will see you coming."

"No matter how early they see me, they will see me kill them in the end." Lee, said, but he knew it was Stile's way of warning and helping him and the other survivors of the complex.

"Whatever you do, make sure you shoot to kill… You need to go and help your friends now." Stiles urged him.

"I may return."

"You will always be welcomed." Stiles assured him.

As Lee flew towards Chicago Randy came up on the radio. "Alicia is hurt, they knew we were coming."

### Indianapolis, Indiana, 30 Minutes Earlier

Randy quickly and brutally killed his remaining two targets. Alicia was just as efficient and met up with him in Indianapolis. Alicia took Randy to the Cardigan building in Chicago arriving there just before midnight.

They changed clothes and entered the skyscraper through the 74$^{th}$ floor office window, one floor above the ballroom.

They casually went downstairs masquerading as a couple attending the dinner.

The security at the main entrance kept a watchful eye on them, but didn't stop them as they entered the ballroom.

They passed the guards, which made Randy uneasy. Surely the guards would ask them who they were, or where they came from, but instead let them inside. They walked around the crowd in the middle of the dance floor, and started to confirm their targets. Alicia was missing two and Randy was missing three. No matter, they had to settle with who were there, because the opportunity would not present itself like this again. Alicia went to the ladies room where one target entered earlier. She easily killed the woman and put her body in the corner of the restroom.

Alicia came out and hailed a guard in frantic panic. "There is a dead woman in there!"

Two guards rushed over as a third reported the situation of the frantic guest to the other guards on duty. Alicia followed the two guards inside, as soon as they entered and turned the corner, Alicia touched both men from behind and killed them. She tossed the men across the restroom like rag dolls ensuring they were not seen from the door entrance. The fate of three more guards ended in like fashion. Randy was outside and ensured the guard remaining outside was led inside by force. The two exited the restroom and split up. Alicia went to the east side of the ballroom while Randy took the south side.

There were metal rail posts in the hallway, which they used by bending them to fit the door handles. In less than a minute, all the double doors except one were barred from the outside of the ballroom.

Randy stepped in and Alicia followed. Randy guarded the door as Alicia went directly to Mr. Huggins, the President of the Cardigan foundation, gave him a hug and instantly killed him when his heart burst from the inside. Randy thought something was wrong because the body guards should have known about the disturbance in the ladies room but yet let Mr. Huggins get hugged. Alicia and several other people exclaimed surprise and fear as Mr. Huggins fell to the ground. Many more people gathered around them and Alicia went person to person killing them as she touched them. It was not until six people and four body guards died that people realized that Alicia was the cause. Alicia sprinted with cat like speed to all the targets except the ones near Randy. People were in a rampage trying to escape out of the room. Randy allowed the people not on the target list to leave, and in less than a few minutes all but five targets were dead.

Alicia and Randy went outside ignoring the terrified fleeing people, and ran for the stairway. Before they could get to the door, gun shots were heard near the elevator. They looked at each other with confusion. Someone was shooting people. Alicia smelled an unfamiliar odor and heard rustling coming from the stairway. "Wait."

"Window" Randy pointed to the window opposite the ballroom doors.

Alicia grabbed Randy around the waist and flew towards the window. She stopped at the window and touched the glass. Randy held on to Alicia's waist from behind allowing her to freely use both hands. The glass shattered and they flew outside high above the city streets.

An armor piercing round hit Randy's arm moving through him and into Alicia's back, lodging itself in her rib cage. She flew and fell downward around the block and then regained control. She flew into the night sky for a few blocks and crash landed on top of 14 story office building.

"Alicia is hurt, they knew we were coming." Randy reported over the radio. Randy kept a hold on Alicia with his good arm and started leaping from building to building until they were out of the city limits.

# Chapter Eight

# Computer Virus

### Fort Knox, Kentucky, 2011

T he Killer Virus was taking its toll on social order and the economy. All military branches and reserve units were deployed or activated in response to the virus's effects. Security was tight at Fort Knox with special attention to sensitive and classified areas and buildings. Mass riots and demonstrations sprung up like wildfire across the nation as people demanded electricity, drinkable water for their homes and businesses, and medication and services for the ill and injured. Word was getting out about the virus nationally and internationally, and many emergency plans were implemented, but it was too slow for most people to see quick and effective results.

Valerie waited uncomfortably pushing against gigantic business cards. It was very dark and cramp inside the pocket of General Hains, but it suited her purpose. General Hains entered the treasury building on a specific mission by the Department of the Army to assess the situation in the Fort Knox area unaware of the miniature hitchhiker. This one of many stops was slow with many security checks and screenings by installation personnel. Valerie's team had to resort to sending her into the area on a leader's reconnaissance confirming the location of the gold and layout of the security system.

It didn't take very long for the general to enter an area near the central vault entrance. As agile as a fly, Valerie flew out of his pocket and up towards a corner opposite a security camera. She immediately whipped out a notepad and sketched out a partially completed floor plan. Room by room she sketched out specific control panels, electric outlets, types of computers, locations of all cameras, motion detectors, pressure sensitive hallways, restrooms and storage rooms. She took out a digital camera and shot pictures without a flash feature. Any dark rooms would rely on her sketches instead of the camera which couldn't create a flash large enough to cover the area. She eventually took the opportunity to hitchhike on top of one of the Soldiers who entered the vault complex and laboriously jotted down the locations of all of the gold bars, including a sketch of the identification access badges into the vaults themselves. The entire process took a little over four hours and another hour until she was able to hitchhike her way back out of the compound. Once outside of the compound, she quickly flew away to rendezvous with her team.

Matthew and Kyle sat at a table in Red Lobster eating their spread of shrimp appetizers as Valerie entered the restaurant. Valerie wore a lavishly decorated dark blue and white business skirt and top. Her brown hair was beautifully coiled up unveiling diamond earrings. She carried a leather brown legal case with a small blue purse at her side. Matthew and Kyle stood up as Valerie approached. Matthew offered her a chair while Kyle looked around wondering why Diana was taking so long in the ladies room.

"Why thank you, Jim." Valerie greeted Matthew.

Mat nodded welcome and eased the chair underneath Valerie.

"So where is Nyota?" Valerie asked.

"She's in the ladies room. I guess I better go see what's holding her up." Kyle replied.

Matthew sat down and waved down a server, then continued to eat his shrimp. Valerie wasted no time and ordered the lunch special and salad bar.

Kyle returned shortly afterwards with a glum expression on his face. "What's wrong Khan?" Valerie asked.

Kyle stopped in front of his chair. "I told you we should not have come here."

"What now?" Valerie asked with a calm demeanor.

"Nyota is arguing with some lady about religion again."

Matthew continued to enjoy his shrimp ignoring the conversation between the two.

"Well it is Sunday, what do you expect when you eat at a restaurant after church is over?"

"Janice, she doesn't have to get into a pissing contest every time she gets approached about God or something similar." Kyle said sitting back down trying to dig into his half eaten plate of crab cakes.

"Oh, let her be, I'm hungry anyways; we can talk about business later."

Matthew smiled as he ate looking up every now and then at the two in front of him. He had not a care in the world knowing the mission could wait while he enjoyed his meal with his wife and only two best friends. He was thankful for meeting them in London almost two years ago. Even Sir Lanhurst, their wealthy exocentric employer was a blessing for them so far. The stainless steel hawk was his latest trade mark establishing his claim of being unstoppable. It was his team which ensured Lanhurst's continued success and future triumph over the obscenely rich upper class.

Valerie looked around the room. "It looks like the virus has brought in a big church crowd today."

"It's a good thing Swiss banks keep better bank records." Kyle stated.

"All you do is think about money." Valerie replied.

"No, that's not true; I think about what money can get me."

Matthew stopped eating and looked at both of them, signing slowly. 'What you have is extra time to be bored because of money. Remember Khan, money cannot buy you dignity, honor or love.'

"Oh boy, another one being ideological."

"He's right Khan, you can't really be happy with money alone." Valerie added.

"What is it with you guys, stomping on my happy dreams. You know, I don't care what you say; a customized Lotus and three girls by the beach will give me all the happiness I can handle."

Matthew smiled, 'And I suppose Nyota is going to let you have a Lotus?'

"What? She's not my mom."

"Who's not your mom?" Diana interrupted as she came up from behind Kyle and placed her hands on top of his shoulders.

Matthew and Kyle stood up as Diana sat down at the table. "You, you're not my mom." Kyle replied and sat down.

Diana stared Kyle down. "I'm your mom if you think I'm going to let you spend half a million dollars on a Lotus just so you can get a few bimbos. Instead, you can give me the money and I will let you have a few grand so you can call an escort service."

Kyle frowned, "The Lotus is for me not the girls."

"Oh, I'm so sorry. I thought for a second there you might want to get laid someday." Diana said with a sarcastic smile.

Valerie and Matthew quietly laughed being accustomed to seeing Diana and Kyle jokingly argue back and forth.

"Like you know what that means."

"Don't go there." Diana warned.

"Only if you leave my Lotus alone."

"Hmm… lucky for you I'm in a good mood today."

Kyle smiled, "When you find the right guy, I will get a Lotus; deal?"

"Deal." Diana returned the smile. "So Janice, is there any good news?"

Valerie finished eating a fork load of salad. "Very."

Diana and Kyle smiled in unison.

'Let's enjoy our meals and talk business later.' Matthew signed.

"A-hum." Valerie mumbled as she ate more salad.

"So what did that lady have to say?" Kyle asked Diana.

"Oh, she wanted to talk about Scientology garbage and the final days of human kind here on Earth." Diana casually said having a Ph D. in World Religions and the Occult.

"What did you do to her?" Kyle asked knowing Diana hated most of the world and didn't care about other people's ideologies.

"I killed her." She nonchalantly replied.

"What?" Everyone's attention went from the food to her.

Diana looked around with an astonished look on her face then smiled. "No, not really. I just numbed her senses for a while. She won't be eating lunch today."

Matthew ate slower a little concerned about Diana. He hoped she would find someone she could love very soon. Having someone to be accountable to, or being mindful of doing good for their sake, kept her out of trouble. It had been three years since Diana killed a person because the man pissed her off arguing about Buddhism. Valerie had to constantly put Diana in check with her therapy sessions for almost a year. Fortunately, Valerie didn't mind and was happy she could use her doctorates in Psychopathology and Pharmacology. In the long run, it was good to know Diana never killed the people close to her, the problem was initially getting close enough to get to know her.

They ate their meals, paid cash, and went back to their base camp at the Galt House Hotel.

# Chapter Nine

# Not as Planned

## South of Chicago, March 18, 2010

The Chicago night air was cool to Alicia as she went in and out of consciousness. Randy had traveled thirty-five miles by the time Lee arrived. Lee's force field engulfed Alicia and Randy and he flew towards Cindy at hypersonic speed. The four came together on top of a water tank in a remote rural area of West Virginia. Lee told Cindy where to manipulate her hand. Cindy spread her body molecules out but was visible to the naked eye. She reached inside of Alicia's back and spread the molecules of the round so that it half floated and fell out of her body. Lee placed his energy rifle on the entry wound and closed it up like a surgical laser. Randy expertly stitched up the cauterized wound.

"What happened?" Cindy asked.

"We got forty-nine, but missed the rest because they never showed." Randy said.

"We need to get home and figure out who survived and why." Lee stated.

Alicia was in pain, so Cindy took her by the hand and they both turned into ghostly figures. In a ghostly state Alicia felt very little pain, mostly that she was weightless and rested. They flew towards Denver with Lee and Randy trailing them. It took the rest of the morning for Cindy to get to the loft. Lee gave Alicia pain medicine which put her out for a few hours.

The three went through the list of survivors. Mrs. Landings was the most influential of the five and was probably the one pulling the strings. Lee told them what Jonah Stiles said about the psychics.

Cindy came up with a crazy idea. "Is it possible that someone wanted us to kill everyone so they could take control of the foundation?"

Randy and Lee thought about that for a moment, and both came up with the same conclusion. Landings might have used the fortune tellers to set up a hostile takeover, but it didn't matter right now, they needed to find the five survivors and kill them as quickly as possible.

Lee kept his backpack on the entire time, which held the power extension of his optics, armor, and weaponry. But he didn't need his armor to detect an ultraviolet laser enter the loft from four blocks away. "They know we're here, sniper at my two o'clock." Lee said and instantly his armor appeared around him. Cindy vanished along with Alicia and Randy.

Lee broke through one of the numerous windows and flew straight to the source of the beam, but never allowed the beam to hit him. He weaved at lightning speed and came on his target before the sniper could barely let off a round. The round shot into the air landing on some unsuspecting location in the city. Lee grabbed the modified 50 Cal and dented the chamber with a slight snap of his fingers. In one motion, he hit the sniper in the head with his rifle and shot his spotter creating a six inch hole in his head.

The sniper was stunned for a moment only to find himself flying through city blocks and crashing into an empty building apartment room.

Lee had an iron hold on the sniper's neck. "Where is Mrs. Landings?"

"I don't know."

"Where is your boss?" Lee asked and ripped off the sniper's radio from his vest chest pocket. The radio was sucked into Lee's armor as if the armor was a living hungry metallic energy field.

"She is storming the building by now."

The sniper's knee caps were destroyed as Lee shot both his knees and flew away back to the loft, leaving the sniper screaming in agony.

Cindy had taken Randy and Alicia to the adjacent building inside a storage room. She could not see what was happening in the loft, but it didn't matter. She would go and investigate on her own not being taxed by having to make two other people invisible and immaterial. Lee was outside and he would take care of the danger. She would soon join him as backup.

Lee approached the loft seeing two dozen soldiers in SWAT uniforms entering the three lofts. There were two other sniper teams in the distance, but this didn't matter to him as he sighted the four men in quick succession seeing through buildings and harden structures. The ultraviolet scopes easily gave them away. His rifle pulsed out hundreds of tight laser beams which penetrated steel, glass, and concrete killing the two teams which were over 200 degrees apart and at different elevations.

Lee looked at the radio frequency hopping setting and immediately cloned it on his helmet station. The radio traffic in Lee's helmet told him that the people in the loft were not aware that they did not have any sniper support, but yet knew something was wrong with the one shot fired at Lee by the probably now unconscious and dying sniper. He scanned for females and found two. One was centered in the rear, so he auto targeted all the other people. They were wearing body plates, but that wouldn't help them.

The mercenaries cleared the area except the outside. Two of them saw Lee fly up twenty feet from the main loft. His rifle shot thousands of lasers into the three lofts leaving total destruction in the path of the beams. The sound of a barrage of invisible burning air pellets could be heard, but no loud bangs or explosive impacts. One female intruder stood in place, while the other laid in the prone. The disbelief on their faces was covered up by their dark tactical visors. All of the male mercenaries were either cut in half or beheaded by the deadly precision of Lee's wrath of laser holes.

Lee paused to carefully aim his rifle this time and shot twice placing a hole into each woman's weapons, and in the process left a half inch hole in the right hand of the woman in the prone. Lee quickly floated into the now windowless loft. "Get up and get next to your friend." Lee commanded as his voice was amplified by this helmet.

"Who's in charge?" Lee waited to see if they were going to play games, he knew already by the radio chatter and the weapons used who was in charge.

Captain Reynolds replied. "I am."

"Where are Landings, Pines, Brown, Connelly, and Nelson?" Lee named all five influential survivors.

"I don't know where they are at this time."

A thin laser beam hit the other woman in the leg creating a small hole an inch deep. She screamed a late scream as the laser cut was so clean that she felt pain a few seconds later.

"Take an educated guess." Lee apathetically commanded.

Captain Reynolds raised her visor; fear reeked through her broken voice, and wide brown eyes. "I only know that they went underground. Mrs. Landings sent me this mission a few hours ago. She might still be in Chicago."

"Leave the radios and your cell phones on the ground. I will let you live today." Lee instructed.

The women were hesitant to leave, fearing they would be shot in the back.

"If I wanted to kill you, I would have done it already. Go before I change my mind!"

Reynolds grabbed the injured woman and they left the loft as quickly as possible stepping on pools of blood and burnt debris. Lee picked up and removed the batteries from the two radios and phones. His armor suit disappeared and revealed his normal human self. "Make me invisible and take me to them." Lee said into the air.

"How did you know I was here?" Cindy asked standing next to him.

"I didn't, but you always have my back as I would have yours." Lee smiled as Cindy made him disappear.

Lee and Cindy appeared in the storage room a minute later. Alicia was much better now and wide awake.

"We need to get to Columbus, Ohio. Cindy do you think you can make all of us invisible with my armor on?" Lee asked.

"How far is that?"

"It's about 1,500 miles, but you shouldn't have to keep it up for more than an hour."

Cindy was not tired, but she would have to spend a lot of energy to be able to cloak Lee's energy field which he needed to protect all of them as they flew past mach 2. "I will try."

"Let's go." Lee opened the storage room door and carried Alicia to a nearby window. Lee turned on his armor and grabbed

Cindy and Alicia by their waists, while Randy held onto Lee from behind. Lee's armor seemed to expand like an ameba engulfing all four people. They disappeared in the hallway and a few seconds later two sonic booms vibrated buildings and homes all around the Denver metro area.

### 1348 Durham St., Columbus, Ohio

An hour later the group landed in the backyard of a secluded home. Lee put away his armor and the four became visible to the naked eye. "I can walk," Alicia said and grabbed Randy's hand.

"Is this where you live?" Randy asked Lee.

"No, this is a FBI safe house." Lee said as he entered a code into a keypad by the sliding opaque glass door, and slid it open.

"Why did we need to come here?" Cindy asked.

"If they have psychics then it doesn't matter, but I am betting that they found us in Denver because Randy or Alicia were identified by someone or the cameras in the ballroom entrance. If Mrs. Landings and her group had died, then the police would have showed up in Denver, and it would have taken them a day to a week for them to knock on your door. So, we should be safe here for a good while, giving us time to figure out where Landings is at." Lee explained as everyone took a seat in the living room.

"I'm sorry I got you all into this mess." Randy apologized.

Alicia massaged Randy's arm and rested her face on his

shoulder.

"I remember the faces of everyone I saw in Yimen. I never told you guys that I stuck around that night. There were several helicopters there shortly after Joshua disintegrated that place. I saw all the security people there, to include Jonah Stiles." Lee recounted and paused, but the three kept silent waiting for Lee to continue. They sympathized with Lee knowing his entire family of eight was killed just so that the foundation would not have to deal with snooping parents or siblings.

"I remember everyone. I wanted so much to jump in there and kill them all." A tear ran down Lee's face. "I didn't have my rifle or armor then. I was too weak to do anything and would have put everyone in danger if I did… I saw nine of those guys back at the loft. I'm glad we didn't get everyone in the ballroom. Now I can kill them all." Lee's anger was aroused.

"If they want a war, I say we give it to them." Alicia solemnly said.

"Cindy, let me know when you are rested so you can get this antibiotic." Lee wrote down the drug name and amount for Cindy so she could go to the pharmacy later and steal it.

"Okay." Cindy took the note, while Lee asked the group what they wanted to eat.

In a matter of a few hours Alicia had her medication, everyone was well fed, and they had a plan of attack on how to track Mrs. Landings by using the phones and radios Lee had acquired.

Randy would call Landings and request a truce by meeting at the Stadium Club US Cellular Field in Chicago. Landings would of course not honor it, but instead try to capture or kill him. Cindy would be there and follow whoever it might be until she got the information the group needed. Cindy was used to spying on people especially mafia bosses, whom she robbed blind, and they could not do anything about it.

The three would be ready to move to wherever Cindy told them to go. The foundation made a very big mistake by creating perfect killing machines. Cindy was invisible to anything, including mind scans. There was probably someone who could detect her presence, but the foundation would not have access to such a person.

The next day, Lee dropped Cindy and Alicia off in Chicago, and took Randy to Joliet along Route 55 to communicate his intentions using Captain Reynolds phone. Landings did not answer but they knew the message would be delivered. Lee and Randy quickly made their way to link up with Alicia half a mile from the Cardigan building. Randy and Alicia held on to the radios which Lee modified so as not to give away their location. Cindy would be the only one who would not be able to listen in on any possible radio traffic, should they be dumb enough to use the same set of frequencies. It really didn't matter. Lee found the tallest building in the area and entered an empty room. He used his rifle to enhance his optical powers and scanned the area around the stadium. He was penetrating miles of structures, which made it very hard to distinguish materials, objects, depth, heat signatures, and distinguishing human physical features. However, he was able to see clear enough to know who was out of place.

Noon came around and spotter teams showed up. There was no radio traffic, but the activity level of ten teams meant that they were very busy identifying everyone in or near the stadium.

Cindy positioned herself twenty paces from the agreed meeting location. Three o'clock came around and Mr. Connelly showed up with an escort of two body guards and a young man who seemed to be tagging along. Cindy quickly moved directly behind the men so she could listen to them down to a whisper.

Mr. Connelly was a short stocky man in his mid sixties, with gray and a mixture of white hair in his full beard. He wore gold framed glasses and a dark blue Armani suit. His Germanic facial features showed a rough but intellectual atmosphere about him. His voice was not deep but not wimpy either.

Lee spotted twelve men armed with side arms and miniature assault rifles converging on Connelly, surrounding him as if they were part of the normal everyday crowd in the restaurant section of the stadium.

It wasn't long before they realized that the meeting was a rouse, or that the over protective security was spotted. The young man next to Connelly made it clear that Randy was not going to show. Cindy realized by his behavior and the things he was telling Connelly, that this was one of the psychics. She wanted to kill the young man and diminish the foundation's psychic advantage, but she had to wait to find the bigger fish.

Connelly ordered everyone to look for anyone spying on them. He specifically asked the young man if he was or would be followed, and the man replied with a weak no. Connelly then ordered everyone to head back to base.

Lee couldn't see details on what was going on in the restaurant area and just kept a watchful eye for any gun fire. There was no activity after a while and the teams he was monitoring moved away from the area. He decided to follow one of the spotter teams and flew in for a closer look.

Cindy flew above Connelly and followed both men to a black HUMMER limousine. She entered the spacious vehicle while Connelly talked to a woman on a cell phone telling her that Randy was a no show. The woman ended the conversation and Connelly just relaxed in the vehicle. It wasn't long before they entered an underground tunnel near the Chicago airport. Connelly and the psychic went through a maze of paved vehicular tunnel strips and a parking area. They exited the HUMMER and entered an underground complex of hallways and rooms, but the targets she was looking for did not reveal themselves. Cindy estimated that there was a battalion of security, logistical, and technician personnel in the complex. She looked for maps or evidence of locations of the other four targets in what seemed to be a command center. Computer screens showed a lot of information on several cities, but it was information in an attempt to locate Randy and the others.

Cindy decided to enter Connelly's office but before she phased through the door, Mr. Pines entered the command center. Maybe this was the break she needed. She went inside the office and watched Connelly work on the computer. He was going over some program records which depicted responses to a

Congressional hearing. Cindy was very interested in the content of the reports and letters Connelly had open on the screen. She wished she could remember like Lee, but it was okay. She would simply wait for the right time and copy a file. Several key names and words popped up at her, two she was familiar with; the SIA, Special Investigation Agency, and CEA, Counter-Espionage Agency. No doubt they would have to answer some very incriminating questions concerning the death of over sixty people to the CEA. They might have been able to cover the deaths in the ballroom and the yacht, but not the ones in the residential homes or in public. The CEA as a federal agency had a reputation to make people talk and to some degree were too powerful. They had legal backing that could override civil rights which spooks only dreamed of. It was the SIA which kept them in check to not completely destroy the freedom of privacy or due process for the nation. Both organizations had their own agenda, but both kept each other in check.

The foundation would be under the microscope and it seemed that the four targets would have to crawl out of their hiding places soon or they would attract unwanted attention. This meant that they would have to eliminate her and the group to be able to go out in public any time soon.

A knock on the door disrupted Connelly, but he continued his work once Mr. Pines entered the office. "Did you hear?" Pines asked.

Connelly paused. "Hear what?"

"Carolyn wants us to move to San Antonio and take the server, and main terminals by tomorrow."

"What! Why?"

"She doesn't want all this hardware to be seen by the CEA, I guess."

"There is no way we are going to be able to do all of that by tomorrow. Why didn't she tell me that when I told her about the no show?"

"I don't know but I don't like the way she said we would be protected. Now those superhumans are out there killing more people." Pines stated as if they were innocent bystanders in the foundation.

"She needs us to keep the books and research straight. So maybe we should be grateful for being alive so far." Connelly commented.

"Well if we can't get all this stuff out of here, she might want to kill us herself." Pines joked.

Cindy stuck around for another forty minutes before Connelly and Pines left the office. She made sure that the computer stayed active and found an empty disk. She copied as much information in the folders she thought were relevant. She quickly went outside of the complex and found a safe location to use her radio without being phase shifted.

Lee had followed the spotter team to the Cardigan building, which meant that activity in the building was business as usual.

They gathered at Alicia's location.

Cindy reported the events, gave them the CD, and

location of the two men. Lee and Randy concluded that Landings may still be in the Cardigan building thinking that the psychics would be able to warn her with enough time to stay safe. The CD had good information on the foundation and their ties with the SIA and CEA, but nothing blatantly illegal. It was highly probable that if the two organizations knew the true activities of the foundation, that they would be their worst enemies and be hit heavy with a hammer of their kind of governmental justice. The foundation was careful not to have hard evidence in the form of data or witnesses to incriminate their activities.

Either way, they were going to conduct their own kind of street justice. Cindy would go look for targets in the building, while the others would go to the complex by the airport and kill everyone there.

An hour later, Cindy entered the Cardigan building lobby and searched for the security room. It was not hard to locate, and she found out where the main offices were for the president of the board. She made her way up to the eighty-second floor. In the main office she found Sheila Nelson lounging on the office sofa. An unfamiliar woman was with her. Cindy waited to see who this second person was, but the woman never talked and just texted on her phone. Cindy went to see what she was texting, but the woman stopped texting once Cindy was at a good vantage point behind her. Cindy noticed that the woman looked around as if she knew Cindy was there, but returned to texting after ten seconds or so.

It dawned on Cindy that this woman might be another psychic. She quickly touched the psychic and spread her body's molecules. The woman turned ghostly and floated down through the sofa and into the floor. Before Shelia knew what was going on, the woman Cindy touched changed into a solid state with half her body fused into the building's structure. Shelia ran towards the door, but only sank into the floor and died as her head was mixed with the wood and concrete floor. The rest of her body exposed to the floor below. Cindy flew through all the rooms on the floor looking for Landings and Brown.

### Cardigan Wheeler Street Complex

The attack on the complex started as all three went straight through the center of the complex from above. Lee created a hole large enough for the three of them to enter, but once they were inside, Lee's optics went haywire.

Alicia and Randy ran around systematically in a clockwise fashion on opposite ends killing everyone they encountered. This gave Lee some time to figure out how to fix his optics. Alicia and Randy killed everyone in the main room to include Mr. Pines, but before they could track down Mr. Connelly, a company of soldiers with complete body armor surrounded the trio. Lee's optics were working perfectly; however, they were being jammed from somewhere in the complex. The company of soldiers fired their arsenal of weapons without warning or discrimination.

Alicia touched the floors and invisible vibrations disintegrated the concrete flooring dropping her into another level below them. Lee stood in between the mercenaries and Randy who followed Alicia into the new hole. Lee returned fire with precision even though his targeting optics was not working. The small caliber rounds hitting Lee's armor did nothing, but the

40mm grenades blew him away from the hole and slightly weaken his energy field.

Lee thought about the soldiers' tactics and rushed the nearest concentration of mercenaries. They didn't seem to care if they were firing into each other with Lee in the middle so he concluded that their disregard to commit fratricide would work to his advantage. The forty by fifty meter control room was completely destroyed by the mercenaries' weapons and Lee's lasers shots. He ran into the mist of the mercenaries and used any mercenary near him as a shield as a few grenades impacted next to him. Lee quickly killed over fifty mercenaries before they stopped flowing into or near the desolate control room. He then ran and jumped into the hole created by Alicia. He passed a series of construction materials into a locker room. Alicia and Randy were nowhere to be found but Lee could faintly smell their scent, which he followed out into a large room filled with a collection of hydraulic machinery which had been automatically shut off when the alarm went out. Lee stood on a balcony rail which led to a hanging walkway around the factory floor. In the distance about twenty feet down he saw an open door. He flew down to the door and the scent was there, confirming Alicia and Randy had entered the visible hallway. His optics were still being jammed which meant either they had an automatic security system which jammed his particular abilities, or it was a trap. Either way he had to find his sister and brother to get out in one piece. The soldiers were a first wave; the second wave would have superhumans or mutants which might be able to hurt him or kill the others.

Randy was reading a schematic of the complex and heard Lee calling their names. Alicia was searching the area several rooms down from Lee, and heard him as well. They both came out of their rooms to see Lee running toward Randy. They gathered around Randy who went back into the room in front of a metal desk.

"We need to get to this section of this room and blow up those tanks which have liquid hydrogen."

"What are they doing with that?" Alicia asked.

"Probably for something with the computers, or some kind of hydrogen based weapon." Lee answered without giving it much relevance, while he looked at the schematic blueprint. It was too convenient that the blueprint was in the room, or maybe it was just laid out because of the foundation moving to another location. It worried Lee a little, but he knew that they would not be expecting what he was planning.

"Are your optics still not working?" Randy asked.

"They are jamming them, but I don't need them to make a hole now, escape to the surface, and try to blow this place up from there, using the hydrogen tanks as a fuel." Lee suggested.

"What if they can jam you after we get out?" Alicia countered.

"That's why I need to make a hole now so you two can get out, and I need to go here." Lee pointed at a large circular structure marked communication node. "They are probably channeling the jamming signal through this location. If I take it out, I should be able to get my optics back."

"I don't like the idea of splitting up in this place." Alicia stated.

"You will only slow me down, and if their best assassin team is here, I will need you guys outside to save my ass if things go wrong."

"I don't like it, but you're right." Randy hesitantly admitted.

"Okay, I will start the hole, Alicia can finish it higher up." Lee said and stepped into the hallway, fired his rifle with a steady wide laser beam straight up. He only hoped that it didn't ignite a flammable fuel or gas line.

Alicia flew up through several floors holding Randy. Lee flew the route on the blueprint and crashed through the communications node door.

### Cardigan International Building, Chicago

Cindy phased through each floor up towards the helipad. She encountered a mess of frantic people running around as the building was being evacuated. Shelia Nelson's dead body had probably given her presence away as someone in the eighty-first floor saw the lower half of two bodies fused with the ceiling. She made it to the rooftop where a bell jet helicopter was started up and ready for takeoff. Cindy could not see the passengers so she flew inside and found only the pilot. She sat in the back and waited patiently.

The familiar face of Mr. Connelly came out of the roof top exit door. The young man who shadowed him followed behind along with Simon Brown, one of the five targets. Mr. Brown was a tall blond skinny man. His business attire and clean cut appearance hinted to his salesmanship and position as an acquisitions specialist. The young man grabbed Connelly's shoulder and stopped him half way to the helicopter.

Cindy flew out of the aircraft and made a beeline for the young man.

"Sir, everything is dark. If you go on that helicopter you will die." The psychic told Connelly.

"So what should I do?"

The psychic looked around at the floor in confusion, "I don't…" he attempted to say as he dropped into the base of the helipad edge. Connelly and Brown saw the man sink into the rooftop, stopping with the top of his head exposed to the city air. Connelly and Brown jumped back in fright. Brown ran for the door but only phased into the door and his body was split in two as the door acted as a divider. Connelly ran in the opposite direction and jumped into the helicopter.

Cindy quickly flew into the helicopter as it took off in a mad rush. She sat down on a vacant seat waiting to see where Connelly would take her.

### Cardigan Wheeler Complex, outskirts of O'Hara Airport

Lee arrived at his destination, but the node seemed to be inoperative. It didn't make sense, the amount of energy required to jam his optics would have to be immense and focused by the use of an antenna or something similar; or if it wasn't directed it would have to be emitted all over the area like an electromagnetic pulse equivalent to a nuclear explosion. Lee looked around and spotted the security camera. He quickly shot it into nothingness.

Lee closed his eyes, relaxed, and just stood with his arms by his side. "Joshua, is this an illusion?"

"Yes," was the mental reply in Lee's head.

Lee opened his eyes and raised his rifle at the center of the room. Laser blasts erupted out of the rifle destroying anything in its path. His optics came back to normal after a few seconds, but the unexpected explosion and concussion from the connecting transformers underneath the room pushed Lee through the door, several room walls, and down the hallway unconscious. His armor deactivated automatically as a reflex to Lee's mental state.

# Chapter Ten

○❖○

# Phase II

S ecurity was quadrupled due to the computer virus, but no amount of security could have anticipated the infiltration of three superhumans on a mission. Valerie held Kyle and Diana by their hands as she flew being the size of an ant into the first set of doors of the main bunker. She flew down the corridor straight into a storage room by the latrines. The trio grew to normal size in the room. Valerie miniaturized herself again and flew into Diana's chest pocket. Diana spread her body molecules looking like a ghost with a bluish and black aura. She wore the colors of a venomous snake; a red, yellow, and black diagonally striped outfit which covered her body and face, but exposed her red hair. She flew into the storage room wall and disappeared from sight.

Kyle turned invisible and walked out of the room and down the corridor. He quickly made his way to the security control room where he stood in a corner watching what was going on.

Mathew waited outside the fort on top of a barracks building about 500 meters away from the initial fence line. He wore attire similar to a ninja, but goggles in place of an open slit. His left arm was colored red and he had a futuristic looking hand gun by his right side. It was twelve inches long and was completely black. There seemed to be no magazine visible and the end of the barrel had a gas suppresser similar to a M60 machinegun. He had left the escape vehicle outside of the Army base and waited patiently as backup in case something went wrong.

Diana flew through the clearance of the ceilings and walls ensuring she didn't expose herself in the open so people wouldn't see her in a ghostly form. The sketches Valerie drew were very precise, including the approximated thickness of structures and walls. Diana made her way to the vault area and quickly disabled the internal cameras on the gold bars and various vaults. She knew that they would take about a minute or more before they sent someone to investigate.

Diana flew to the center of their collection point. Valerie flew out of Diana's pocket and increased in size to normal, but she had a desk size cylinder coiled with pure silver by her side. It had a black box on top with a simple on/off switch and a safety latch.

Diana quickly flew to the outer extremes of stacked gold bricks. She placed a metallic disk on top of the stack and flew off to the next stack going through the sealed rooms. Valerie did the same in the opposite direction. Fifteen stacks were tagged before half a minute elapsed. Diana turned on the cylinder and it hummed of electric static.

Valerie flew to the outer stack touched it and it automatically turned into the size of a speck of sand. She picked up the speck with her finger and placed it in a small metal box she held in her other hand. Diana called off the time at thirty-seven seconds as Valerie placed the second gold stack in her metal box. At fifty seconds Valerie was on her last stack. She flew back to the cylinder and placed the small metal box on top of it. The box clung to the cylinder like a magnet. Diana stood next to Valerie as she and the cylinder shrunk to the size of a Nat once again. Diana opened her pocket and Valerie flew inside it carrying the cylinder.

Kyle watched the security guards monitor the security vault cameras go black. They started their normal procedures for a technical issue and the required investigation of the vault. There were five Soldiers in the camera room, but before the word could be put out on the land line the Soldier was knocked out from an invisible blow to the neck. Before the other four Soldiers could react, they fell to the ground unconscious or paralyzed. Kyle made another round and knocked out any would be recovering conscious Soldiers. He turned off the monitors except for one which was covering the center of the vault. Once the monitor returned to normal and showed an empty vault except for a stainless steel hawk statue, he turned that monitor off. He left the security room and quickly headed to the storage room. He arrived at the storage room before the women.

Once the three were together, they quickly left the bunker the same way they arrived. Valerie flew towards Mathew and allowed Kyle and Diana to return to normal size. She then flew into Mathew's pocket, who leaped his way to the getaway vehicle. Kyle and Diana made their way to the hotel on their own powers, while Mathew and Valerie drove their Lexus an hour away to a warehouse in Portland, Tennessee.

They entered the warehouse and Valerie quickly off loaded her payload being the size of a hummingbird in a pre-designated location on the warehouse floor. A specially constructed eighteen wheeler truck, able to take the load of so much gold, occupied half of the building. Mathew ensured the warehouse was locked and secure. All windows on the property were painted dark blue and adjacent properties were leased out to bogus companies. Private security patrolled those properties as preventive measures to keep criminals away from the area. The warehouse itself was not covered by the Burns International Security company, but it was monitored by fake cameras and preprogrammed lights at night.

Valerie spread all fifteen 10 x 10 x 6 foot stacks of gold bricks on half of the warehouse floor. In a matter of a few seconds, the gold, pallets, and metal tags enlarged to their normal size. The total amount of gold stolen was worth approximately $20 billion dollars. The bricks of gold were sprawled out all over the floor covering the pallets on large piles of loose bricks.

Valerie ran into a side office and changed clothes as Mathew started to place the gold bricks in specially constructed boxes. Valerie came out of the office wearing jeans and a nature lover T-shirt. She assisted Mathew as they filled the metallic boxes with retractable four inch metallic wheels. It took a few hours but they uploaded the gold in the flat bed which was specially made to hold the weight and size of the metallic containers so as not to shift on its base. They gathered all the pallets and pallet debris into one area and then stuffed them into a large metal container. Mathew picked up the container, weighing a thousand pounds, and placed it inside the truck. The people who were going to pick up the gold were also going to dispose of the pallet evidence. Mathew made a quick sweep of the warehouse floor and rooms to make sure no evidence of them being there was found. His keen senses didn't see everything down to the atom, but they were strong enough to see down to hair fibers, skin oils, and microscopic droplets of any kind.

Valerie opened the warehouse door while Mathew drove the truck out. She then got into the Lexus and followed Mathew. They drove to Amarillo, Texas with no incidents, which included stopping at weighing stations where Valerie had to shrink the containers in the back in order to take the weight off of the truck. Valerie flew out of the truck before Mathew entered an auto factory and parked it inside the factory floor which had one of its garage doors open. The factory seemed to be abandoned, but it was simply empty as if everyone who worked there had taken the day off work or gone to lunch. Mathew left the keys in the cab and walked away from the parked truck. He left the factory and was promptly picked up by Valerie along the street side. They left immediately for Nevada where their next heist was awaiting. Mathew and Valerie drove into a Las Vegas junk yard where the Lexus was quickly scraped by the owner of the establishment. Mathew did not need to say anything except give the person in charge his keys and a silver dollar.

In exchange the owner gave Mathew keys to a used motorcycle. The couple took off on their new vehicle straight to Alamo on route 93. It was late in the second day of their traveling when they met with Diana and Kyle. The house they were given was comfortably stocked with furnishings and provided extra land for needed privacy from neighbors.

They each were given $450 million into their respected offshore accounts in a matter of a week. They knew that the gold hadn't been fenced off that fast, and the money was coming from Sir Lanhurst's personal assets. The gold would have to be melted down and then filtered to be cleaned from distinguishing elements as being from Fort Knox. Once melted, it would have to be distributed in small amounts as not to attract attention. In the big picture of fencing, it was not their concern as long as they got paid for their workmanship.

## Chapter Eleven

# Only Two Remain

### Cardigan Wheeler Complex, outskirts of O'Hara Airport

T he factory pumped millions of liquid plastic material into specially designed molds and shapes. The machinery had been turned off and half created gadgets were placed on hold. Lee awoke in the middle of the factory floor strapped to one of many metal vertical 16"x16" beams in the structure. A dozen soldiers surrounded him with assault rifles at the ready. His armored suit was not on him, and he could feel the metal-like material from his bonds cutting into his wrists. He couldn't see what was holding his hands behind his back in between his body and the metal beam, but he sensed they were medium quality handcuffs. His chest and legs were strapped to the beam with several thick plastic bands. His black thick slakes and collared cotton short-sleeve brown shirt didn't give him any comfort or protection. His backpack was on a table in the distance, while a man searched its contents. A very well geared and notably fit soldier stood in front of Lee with a knife in his right hand. "Who are you?" The soldier asked with his helmet and visor still on.

"Who are you?" Lee replied.

The soldier plunged the knife into Lee's side. The tip hit a rib and slipped past stopping short of penetrating his left lung. He turned the blade and moved it up Lee's side scrapping three rib bones. Lee moaned in pain, but clenched his teeth together staring down the soldier's visor. The brown shirt was heavily stained with blood, but not much as a normal person. Lee's body seemed to create blood clogs on the wounds almost immediately. The partial reflection of Lee's face and the soldier's dark eyes through the visor somehow gave Lee strength. "Answer the question." The soldier commanded.

"I'm Simon Recker." Lee made up a name.

"Who else is with you?" The soldier asked as he started to move the knife downward in a zigzag pattern.

"Just those two..." Lee groaned.

The soldier removed the knife from Lee and stepped back, turned around and walked towards the table with Lee's backpack.

"Sir, there are two books, pens, pencils, and a laptop, which I can't seem to open." The man at the table reported.

The officer turned back around as his attention was diverted to sounds behind Lee. Lee heard moment of people, he estimated maybe five to seven people moving towards him. The officer stood ten paces from Lee and motioned the people behind Lee to approach. "Let's find out who's telling the truth. Bring them here."

Two soldiers each carried Alicia and Randy by hands and feet. Their hands and ankles were cuffed together by heavy duty metallic cuffs. Both had their mouths gagged, but Alicia was visibly unconscious. The soldiers threw the couple on the hard floor as three other people followed them and came into Lee's view. There was a two soldier escort and another person who was not a soldier, but wore a SWAT jacket. It was a white Caucasian man in his late 50s with short gray and black hair thinning out on the top of his head. His mustache and beard was short and trimmed nicely. He did not have a weapon, but perhaps it was covered by the jacket. Lee could not tell and that sort of bothered him since his senses were somehow stiffened, but it didn't matter at the moment considering the situation. Either this man was one of the superiors or in all probability one of the few superhumans working for the foundation.

The lead soldier grabbed Alicia by the hair and picked up her head so her face was visible. Randy twisted his neck with to side of his head slightly lifted off the floor, to see what the soldier was doing and to look at Lee. His facial expression of pain and anger could be felt by Lee as they helplessly stared at each other.

"I don't suppose she will be talking soon?" The soldier looked at the older man in the SWAT jacket, and let go of Alicia's hair allowing her face to flop hard on the concrete floor.

"I can relieve her if you like." The older man replied.

The lead soldier stepped up next to Randy, kneeled down and grabbed him by the neck with one hand and with the other held his knife up to Randy's face. "What says you, should we wake her up so she can see you scream like a little baby?"

Randy spoke calmly, but the only thing that could be heard was a calm muffled sound as the he was still gagged.

The soldier placed the tip and blade under the gag and cut it off Randy's face, in the process leaving a knife cut on his cheek. "What did you say?"

Randy spit out the remains of the gag from his mouth, "I said, wake her up." His eyes showed no fear, and his half smile demonstrated contempt.

The lead soldier looked at the telepath. "You heard the man, wake her up."

The telepath touched Alicia on the head and about ten seconds later, Alicia woke up in a drowsy state.

The lead soldier kept his hold on Randy's neck but placed the blade of his knife on Randy's shoulder.

Lee assessed every detail he could about his surroundings and the twenty-one enemy targets in front of him. He might be able to break from his cuffs and ties, but the soldiers aiming their weapons on him would have enough time to react and shoot him. Without his armor, he would not be able to withstand the lethal bullets, but he always had hope. Perhaps Alicia or Randy would be able to distract the soldiers so he could get loose and get to his back pack - perhaps.

Alicia finally came to her senses, looked around, and sat up off the floor. One of the soldiers stuck the muzzle of his rifle on her chest. "It's okay." The lead soldier said, and the guard over

Alicia stepped back but kept his rifle muzzle three feet away and trained on her center of mass.

"If you answer correctly, I will be generous and kill you quickly. Now, who else is with you besides you three." The soldier looked at Alicia while he moved the edge of his knife under Randy's neck.

"Joshua." Alicia simply replied.

The lead soldier looked at the telepath. The telepath nodded slightly and said nothing. Alicia thought quickly and came up with the conclusion that this man next to her was a telepath.

"Well, the great Joshua." The lead soldier started to say as the telepath interrupted. "She knows I can read her mind."

Lee cleared his mind and so did Randy and Alicia. It was a reflex on their part knowing what to do having trained in the foundation, and with Joshua's guidance. The telepath turned towards the lead soldier. "They are all clearing their minds."

The lead soldier bowed his head in frustration. "I guess the interrogation is going to be done my way." He stuck his knife deep into Randy's stomach.

Randy screamed in pain, and broke the cuffs on his wrist. He was about to slice off the lead soldier's arm off when his muscles failed to respond to his commands.

The telepath's paralyzing mental hold on Randy was too much for him to take. The lead soldier looked at Randy and mocked him as he pushed him off and stood up. "So you think you can hurt me?"

A loud but very short scream reverberated through the massive room. The telepath's entire right leg up through his chest and right side of his head flopped to the ground like jelly dragging the rest of his seemingly normal body with him. Alicia's hand was touching the telepath's right foot as the guarding soldier shot her two times in the chest. The rounds exited her back leaving two very large exit wounds. She had disintegrated the cuffs and also the telepath but paid a heavy price.

Lee started to break his bonds but stopped instantly as he noticed that three soldiers kept a watchful eye on him. Lee being shot now would not help anyone, and even though Alicia was dead, Randy would have the best chance of saving himself and Lee at the moment.

Randy sprung into the air with his ankles still cuffed and plunged his fist into the lead soldier's chest plate, while grabbing the soldier's arm with his other hand. The Kevlar plate caved into the soldier's chest causing blood to spew out of his mouth, eyes, and ears. Six soldiers fired at Randy, hitting mostly the lead soldier and whatever else was in the path of the rounds as even one soldier was hit in the foot by a stray round in the cross fire. Randy used the lead soldier as a shield as he leaped for the table where Lee's backpack and laptop laid.

Lee saw his chance as now all the soldiers were focused on Randy's lethal commotion. He put all the strength he had on his arms and legs breaking the straps around his legs, arms, and cuffs on his wrists. A soldier saw Lee break free and turn his weapon in Lee's direction.

Randy's heroic feat of holding the lead soldier as a shield lasted only long enough for him to reach the table where the soldier at the table had now pulled out a side arm 9mm and started firing at Randy. Randy took a round to his shoulder while two other rounds missed him and hit the floor. The shoulder pain was added to his stomach wound and a bullet hitting his hip from one of the soldiers in the perimeter. Randy swung at the Soldier's hand shattering his bones and loosening the pistol from his grasp. Randy released the lead soldier and grabbed the laptop. He flung it in the direction of Lee and then tried to grab the lead soldier again, but two more rifle rounds hit Randy in the left leg and arm.

Lee's wrists were slightly bleeding from the hardened metal edges cutting into his skin as he broke free. He pushed with all his might against the beam propelling himself towards Randy and the table. Lee dove for the incoming laptop while a few plastic straps around Lee's feet kept him from smoothly gliding to his destination. Six soldiers changed targets and aimed their rifles at Lee as he touched the flying laptop in mid air. The rifles erupted with bullets as the laptop transformed into a liquid metal upon touching Lee and engulfed him with his energy metallic armored suit. A round braised through Lee's right calf before the armor could fully cover him. The twenty or so rounds fired at Lee hit the armor and bounced off or mushroomed in place falling to the ground at various angles.

Randy fell to the ground having suffered major damage to his body, but the hail of fire which initially hurt him was diverted towards Lee by this time. Lee felt the burning pain of the wound to his leg, but anger and adrenaline had taken over. His armored suit disintegrated the plastic straps and stopped the bleeding to his calf, ribs, and wrists. He leaped next to Randy but didn't stop there, grabbing his backpack which immediately was absorbed by his armor. Two energy rifles seemed to emerge from the armor attached to each hand as if the backpack was transformed into added weaponry. Lee flew twenty feet away from Randy and turned around facing all the soldiers, Randy and Alicia.

Lee's optics targeted every soldier and in less than three seconds laser blots shot out of his weapons at full auto beheading or completely destroying all twenty soldiers riddled with hundreds of three inch holes, leaving a stench of burnt flesh and blood everywhere. The air in front of Lee sizzled as the heat produced by the origin of the blots emitted a slight thunder sound as laser light forcefully split air atoms. Lee scanned around looking for any reinforcements, but none came. His rifles were absorbed by his armor as he flew next to Randy and looked at his injuries with his optics. Randy had a punctured liver and intestine, a round in his shoulder, both lungs were punctured, and a flesh wound to the arm, but the most damaging injury was his femoral artery which was severely ruptured. Not even with his lasers could he stop the bleeding, since the rupture was too long and deep in the hip area.

"Finish what we started." Randy weakly and painfully said as Lee held Randy's head up.

Lee's helmet didn't disappear, but his visor turned transparent so Randy could see Lee's face. "I promise brother, I will."

"Take care of…" Randy started to say but stopped and slowly fell unconscious.

Lee knew that Randy would not wake up. "I will take care of Cindy." Lee said as if talking to a live audience. Lee stood up and walked up to Alicia's dead body. He stared at his sister and brother for a short while. Tears ran down Lee's face as he fired a wide laser beam for about half a minute at Randy and Alicia, burning them into almost ashes. Radio traffic started to come up on Lee's helmet station. He was still in the complex, but the chatter was concerning an alarm at the Cardigan building. The adrenaline had worn off and Lee's leg ached badly. He hovered in mid air taking the weight off his leg, looked all around him and picked a point above him. He smiled knowing that Cindy must be giving them hell, now it was his turn to do the same. He flew and fired his rifle in the direction of travel and ended up outside next to the far perimeter of the airport with the sunlight peering through an evening cloudy sky overhead. His optics was working perfect now and he could see the volatile areas of the complex. He carefully aimed his rifle and fired at the areas causing the complex to explode inside itself destroying the complex and killing about 75% of the people inside as the majority of the complex caved in or burned uncontrollably. He focused carefully all around the complex again and in less than a minute he sniped and killed the remaining occupants in the complex. He knew that Mr. Pines was dead, and the rest would not be in the complex or if they were he had just killed them.

The radio chatter had stopped with the destruction of the complex, but he homed in on the transmissions from the Cardigan building as he sped off at below supersonic speed so as not to alert them of his approach.

Lee arrived at the building only to see Cindy's handiwork

on the 82$^{nd}$ floor and the helipad. "Three down, two to go." Lee said to himself. He then looked back in the direction of the airport and concluded that the helicopter that was not on the helipad was probably headed to the airport. He did not see a helicopter, but that was normal because at that distance and not knowing the helicopter's flight path it was like finding a needle in a hay stack. He flew towards the airport this time breaking the sound barrier.

### O'Hara International Airport, Chicago

Cindy waited patiently as the helicopter approached the airport. She noticed that Mr. Connelly was very agitated before the helicopter skids touched the ground. She could not hear what was being said on the internal headphones of the craft, but Connelly was very angry. He practically jumped out of his seat and started to run on the pavement screaming at the top of his lungs. "You witch! Come back!" he yelled as he saw his ride taking off in the distance.

It was a futile attempt as the helicopter rotors drowned out most of his angry rambling screams, but Cindy clearly heard it and knew that Mr. Connelly had used up his usefulness. Cindy grabbed Mr. Connelly by the shoulders as she flew next to him, made him invisible and phased at the same time. She went up through and above the moving rotors. Mr. Connelly felt his body lift off the ground as if weightless and like a ghostly figure move through the helicopter rotor's edge and oriented upside down. To his dismay, he saw his body materialize back to normal and his weightlessness disappear. He fell head first down into the spinning rotor blades and his doom.

Cindy flew as fast as she could towards the Learjet which Mr. Connelly was so frantically trying to hail. She got half way to the runway, when she realized that she could not over take the jet by herself. She turned her body back to normal, and used the radio Lee gave her.

"Lee, Mrs. Landings is the last one and is on a jet that just took off from the airport. I need you." Cindy called for help.

A sonic boom hit the airport as Lee seemed to appear almost in a sudden stop in front of Cindy. "Where is the plane?" Lee simply asked not wanting to waste time.

"Pick me up and let's go that way." She pointed, a little surprised that he was there at the airport almost instantly.

Lee and Cindy quickly caught up with the Learjet twenty miles to the northeast. Lee flew above the jet and scanned all occupants. His armor absorbed all radar emissions, making him invisible to air traffic control or onboard aircraft radars. The pilots and passengers of the plane were ignorant to the superhumans looming above them. There were two females, a male passenger, and the two pilots. Lee thought carefully before taking action. Mrs. Landings was no fool; the other female was probably a psychic or telepath. Or both a telepath and psychic were onboard. He could shoot the plane and kill everyone, but the plane would crash into Michigan Lake and for all he knew the pilots maybe innocent pawns only performing a service they grew up and learned to do. He could go inside the plane, but if there was a telepath ready for them, then there was a chance that Cindy or he would be severely harmed or killed.

Lee's armor linked Cindy to his helmet station. "Cindy, I need you to confirm Landings is on the plane and her exact location. Once I know that, I can kill all the passengers and leave the pilots to safely land the plane. If I scan the passengers a telepath might know that I can see them, so I will take you to the plane, you go inside and just look around then drop out of the plane."

"Okay I will try" Cindy said a little hesitant not ever having to phase through objects moving over 300 mph.

Lee headed to the front just before and above the pilot compartment. He held Cindy as she touched the plane and sunk through the fuselage. Lee quickly flew up getting some distance from the plane as not to alert any telepath that there was a person outside of the plane.

Cindy melted through the wall of the plane, and then she stopped phasing and stood inside the plane. She turned towards the passengers and saw her target. As quickly as she entered the plane, she exited below it and waited for the plane to get some distance before turning visible again.

Lee spotted Cindy low and far behind the plane and swooped down to get her. His armor once again enveloped her and they speed off after the jet.

"Landings is on the left side seat."

"Roger." Lee replied as he flew directly above the pilot compartment turned to face the plane with Cindy on his back and targeted the passengers with his rifle. Very fine laser beams penetrated the plane and killed the three passengers, Landings being the last target. The lasers also penetrated the center auxiliary fuel tanks deep underneath the floor and ignited the jet fuel. The plane turned into a ball of fire as Lee flew out of harm's way.

"What happened?" Cindy yelled.

"Damm… Hold on!" Lee replied as he flew parallel to the fiery plunging and exploding plane. His optics showed the trajectory of flight and plotted a projected crash point into Lake Michigan. There were no water vessels in the area so the plane would not kill any more people besides the pilots if they were not already dead.

"It's okay, it will crash in the lake." Lee stated.

"Was she the last one?" Cindy asked not knowing what happened to Randy or Alicia, thinking they were still somewhere killing targets or something.

Lee grabbed Cindy and moved her to his front as they flew southward. "Cindy, Alicia and Randy are dead."

"What? How?" Cindy could not believe her ears as she started to sob and hug Lee tightly.

Lee quickly made it to the coastline, landing in a secluded area of wilderness by the water. Lee explained what happened to the best of his knowledge while they sat together on the sandy and rocky shore facing the lake.

They sat silent for a while before Cindy told Lee everything that she had done, and even though all the people they wanted dead had died, the cost of revenge was painfully engraved in them both.

Lee's discomfort in his leg increased, even though his armor field was surrounding his calf. The internal nerve endings were being numbed to a point and the injured area was starting to affect the rest of the leg. Lee massaged the surrounding area gently looking for any internal bleeding with his optics as his helmet visor appeared on his head while they sat. "Is it bad?" Cindy asked realizing for the first time that he was wounded.

"I don't see any internal bleeding, but a chunk of muscle was torn off. It will heal in time, but I'm going to have a very big scar." Lee casually replied.

"Lee, what do we do now?" Cindy sadly asked putting her hands on her face and massaging her eyes while her knees supported her elbows.

Lee looked out into the horizon with his optics disappearing from in front of his face and eyes. "Joshua, help us."

Cindy stopped massaging her eyes and wiping the dry tears from her cheeks. A fairly young man stood on the water with worn blue jeans and a collared gray and white striped shirt. His glossy black hair seemed very silky flowing down two inches short of his shoulders. His beard was short and he had handsome bone structure. His piercing blue eyes were strong but yet gentle with a confidence and absolute peace which made your heart pause to enjoy the moment. He walked on the water and onto the shore stopping one foot from the two and kneeled.

"I am here my beloved son and daughter." Joshua said holding out his hands so that they both could touch him.

Cindy stared at him and then at his hand as she touched it with hers, not believing that she was touching Joshua for the first time. Lee grabbed Joshua's hand as well but he was not astonished with wonder, he was at rest now, feeling a huge weight taken off his chest. "Is it really you?" Cindy asked.

"Randy and Alicia…" Lee interrupted.

"Yes it is me. I am sorry for Randy and Alicia, but all of you made your decisions." Joshua replied and sat down facing them with legs crossed.

"Can't you bring them back?" Cindy hopefully asked.

"If I did, would someone around the world be required to forfeit their lives in their place?" Joshua countered.

"What do you mean?" Cindy asked.

"If he brought Randy or Alicia back to life, their future actions will affect the lives of other people, death or life, good or bad would be the result." Lee answered.

"So you see; when I became who I am now, I didn't bring back my wife and daughter because changing the past also changes the future. I could change anything, but then where is your free choice if I change things for one person and then not the other, or myself for that matter. This is why I do not change the past or bring back things from the past into the present. I change the future with actions in the present, not the past." Joshua explained while they listened intently.

"When you ask me for something I can give you, you decided on what you asked for, I simply give you what you ask for out of my loving heart, and your free choice. Randy and Alicia are in a better place... It is not easy for you to understand at the moment, but I assure you that they are with me and are happy now."

"So, what now?" Cindy asked disappointed.

"The foundation will be dismantled by the government. They will never bother either of you or harm anyone else. Evil is everywhere, and the foundation was only a single rain drop in a midsummer rain shower. I will help you every day of your lives, but it is up to you to decide to fight injustice and fight as hard as you wish, not me."

"Joshua..." Lee started to say.

Joshua looked at Lee. "Yes, Lee."

"You know people's hearts. So can you see if any of the family members of all those people we killed can be helped in some way?" Lee asked.

"I will see to it that insurance policies are created or fulfilled, that people get proper medical treatment, and that relationships are mended and flourish. Is that what you mean?" Joshua said.

Lee grinned slightly. "Yeah. Oh, can you do something about my calf?"

"Sure." Joshua smiled and Lee's calf, rib, and wrist wounds were instantly made whole with no evidence of injury. His clothes were completely mended, and armor was also turned off by Joshua as if he had the master switch.

"Thanks." Lee said feeling normal again.

"So we go back to our homes and jobs?" Cindy asked not knowing how the future was going to play out.

"Well, you can, but I suggest you two travel and not stay in one place too long. You are both going to run into the one person that you will fall madly in love with." Joshua replied.

"Really?" Lee interrupted knowing that it would take a very special person to put up with his unique personality and baggage.

"Yes, really. You won't see it coming, even with your super vision." Joshua smiled.

"Well, I hope my man can cook, because I don't want to wake up without a person to share breakfast with." Cindy joked.

Lee looked at her. "Don't worry sis, now that I know exactly how this destiny thing works, I will ask for a fully cooked breakfast every morning and holiday meals every year, so you won't have to lift a finger." Lee laughed, staring at Joshua.

"My thoughts exactly." Joshua smiled and stood up.

Lee and Cindy also stood and they hugged each other saying their good-byes.

Joshua faded away into thin air, while Lee flew off with Cindy to Washington, D.C. They arrived that night to a house owned by Cindy. Lee spent several days there with his sister, wanting to spend quality time with her before he went to wherever he was going. It was a heartfelt good bye when the day came for Lee to leave, flying off towards the setting sun.

Cindy wasn't sure of what to do, but Seattle seemed to be calling her name, so she made arrangements to move there as soon as possible leaving D.C. without regrets.

## Chapter Twelve

O❖O

# The Ultimate Heist

M any people were working feverishly on the tar mat outside Area 51 hangar 22. Several aircraft were being moved in the wake of the computer virus as the virus made its way into the secure servers catering to the complex. Special care was taken to have the onboard computers and communications systems turned off or disabled. All crafts were grounded and stored in hangars, while the rest of the activities in the area continued on high alert due to the virus and possible terrorist threats or attacks. There were several F-35 Lightnings on the grounds and the team would have their pick. Stealing a stealth fighter was a feat in itself, but stealing it in plain sight with people all around was almost an impossible task, but it was a task the team was very eager to attempt.

Due to superhumans publicly coming out in the form of superhero groups with governmental backing and demonstrating their abilities, there were special measures taken in top secret technology focused installations. Area 51 was one of these installations with its perimeter being monitored by live patrols, motion sensors, specialized optical sensors, radar, and bio scanners. The team would have to figure out how to defeat the detection systems before they could even get close to the hangars. Once in, they could disable the systems and then it would be easier leaving than getting in. However, unlike the Fort Knox gold bricks, there were more variables to consider and the stealth fighter would have to be shrunk down into one useful piece of machinery and moved over twenty miles of clear Nevada terrain before it could be blended in with civilian traffic.

"I think I can get all of us in this hangar without being detected that is if Mathew is right about the transport." Diana pointed at one of twenty-two hangars on a satellite photo of the complex displayed on a large monitor screen.

'The aircrafts that normally fly in and out are grounded, so I am sure they will have more ground transports moving on a regular basis. We just need to tag along in one of them.' Mathew signed.

"I don't like not having a leader's recon." Valerie stated.

"It should be okay. I can scout around and let you guys know what is going on, once inside." Kyle assured her.

'We will be blind going in, but we won't be once inside. One or two fifteen minute recons are good enough for what we need.' Mathew added.

"The badge is what I'm worried about." Kyle said. "We won't have time to make a real fake badge, and even then a badge might not work."

'It is only a distraction, and if all goes as planned none of us will need a badge or have to talk to anyone there.' Mathew countered.

'So are we set?' Mathew asked the team having rehearsed the heist for the twentieth time.

"Yeah I'm good." Diana replied.

"Me too." Kyle said.

"Ditto." Valerie said.

'Okay, let's get some sleep. Wake-up is at 16:00 hrs.' Mathew finalized.

They slept that afternoon until 15:30 hrs. Mathew was the first one up and Valerie and Kyle ate a specially prepared protein and vitamin meal. They didn't need to eat for a very long time, but the special meal provided a means to keep them from going to the restroom for a few days and hunger for a week. Mathew and Diana didn't need to eat at all, and ate only for the pleasure of tasting food. The only stops they would be having were for changing vehicles and one gasoline stop. By 17:00 hrs they were on the road to their staging point off along Extraterrestrial Highway 375 northeast of the airfield. The vehicle they used to get there was abandoned 50 meters from the highway, sterilized, and buried fifteen feet into the sand with the help of Valerie's and Diana's special touch. They had changed into their thieving costumes. All had dark flat black goggles, and for the most part they wore ninja outfits. Mathew had his right arm colored red, the rest was black, and he wore a sidearm, a futuristic pistol, similar to a Logan's Run movie. Diana's costume was riddled with small red, black, and yellow stripes. Valerie's ninja suit was all dark brown, why Kyle's was completely black.

Valerie shrunk herself, Mathew, Diana, and their equipment. They hitched a ride in Kyle's specially made compartment on the side of his belt. Kyle turned invisible and flew along the roadways towards a perimeter security gate. No vehicles had passed by the time he arrived to the gate, but it didn't matter. He landed on the inside of the gate next to the main bunker. There were fifteen security guards on duty all wide awake and attentive to their surroundings. Four vehicles were parked behind the bunker which was used for a hot pursuit or maybe for checking out intruders near the gate fence line. They were similar to armored Hummers, but a little larger and flatter. If Kyle didn't know any better, he would have thought they were supped up and could give street racers a good run for their money.

Kyle stepped inside of the main bunker which could see oncoming traffic. He spotted what he was looking for on the far wall. It was 18:42 hrs and Valerie would need to rest in about an hour or so. Hopefully, a vehicle would come by soon, if not he would have to fly into the airfield by himself which might alert the bio scanners between the gates and the field. Being in a vehicle cleared to enter the complex full of living passengers was the best camouflage, and hopefully their timing was good. He walked around looking at every detail about the security and people there. The guards were very well armed with side arms, assault rifles, sniper rifles readily available, Mark-19s mounted on two vehicles, and M2 .50 Caliber machineguns mounted on the other two. They all had communication headsets and wore medium body armor. They acted as if they were in a war zone, and it was clear to Kyle they would shoot first, shoot again, and ask questions later.

Kyle waited impatiently trying to gather as much information of what was going on by listening to the radio traffic in the bunker. Security checks were reported, civilian and military chatter was being monitored but not much was happening. Kyle walked up behind a guard sitting at a console, and then it dawned on him to look at the security log. He could make out a scheduled entry of a bus or truck at 19:15 hrs. He would be cutting it close if he waited for the vehicle to pass, but knowing the level of security, the vehicle would not be late. If the vehicle was late or even early, it would be stopped and checked or not allowed to enter. This kind of delay would not be desired by the driver or people waiting on the transport, so chances were that it would be on time. Kyle waited and before he knew it, the time of no return had passed. To his relief a bus approached with headlights on. The setting sun created a red sky to the west while the bus sped towards the gate. The security guards prepared the gate to be opened and the mobility barriers to be lowered. Kyle walked outside thinking the bus was going to slow down, but to his surprise the bus driver not once touched the brakes. Kyle quickly flew towards the bus and turned around fifty meters outside of the gate. He gave the bus some space and flew in the same direction of travel matching the bus's speed as it screamed past the opened security gate. He flew onto the top front of the bus, holding on to the leading edge as the bus traveled towards the airfield at 80 mph.

Kyle estimated that twenty minutes had elapsed since the bus passed the gate and could see the hangars and airfield in the distance, but he worried that Valerie would not be able to keep her guests and equipment shrunk for very long. She would normally be able to keep herself shrunk for about five hours, but people were different since they had biological forces at work and it took more energy out of her to be able to keep people shrunk for long periods. Either way, he saw his target and waited for the right time to release the bus as it headed to the south end of the field. He kept low to about four feet above the ground and followed the pavement making sure he flew over traffic areas and not over the grass or what seemed to be unused pavement by vehicles.

The tar mat was now dark, even the outside lights were dimly lit with blue lighting. White light was being used in the distance where the bus was headed, and it seemed that white light was also used inside the hangars which were specifically designed not to allow light to escape. Kyle knew this by the way white light came out only when the hangar main doors were opened. The targeted hangar was closed so he would have to go to one that was open and find a secluded room. The adjacent hangar was partially opened with people moving in and out as if it was a factory floor in full operation.

Kyle quickly flew inside and paused for a moment as he saw what seemed to be a room he could use to drop his team off, but what delayed him was an aircraft he was not familiar with. It looked like an F-35, but this one was a little bigger and had two oval exhausts. It seemed to be an advanced prototype by the looks of its construction, but Kyle came back to his senses and focused on his job. Many technicians and engineers were in the hangar bay, but he was able to open and close the door to a storage closet without anyone noticing. There was very little room but he made himself visible which was the team's queue to come out of his protective belt.

The three team members grew to normal size, almost suffocating Kyle between them and the door. Diana instantly dematerialized and floated into the floor giving the other three space to move around in the tight room. Mathew sensed that they were not in the right hangar. "Where are we?" Mathew whispered in the black room.

"The adjacent hangar to the southwest. I couldn't slip into the hangar because it was closed up. This hangar has some weird plane thou." Kyle whispered back and turned invisible.

"How do you feel darling?" Mat whispered again.

"Tired, but I will be good in a few minutes." Valerie whispered back.

"When Venom gets back she will take us inside the hangar. Sia, you scout around for the control tower and security center." Mathew said and waited for Diana to return.

Diana was gone no more than two minutes. "This isn't the hangar, but they got some really cool plane in this one with like fifty people all over it." Diana reported.

"I'm sure we would have been sent to steal it if people knew about it, but that doesn't matter. Venom, take Hummel and me to the other hangar. Sia will scout around. In twenty minutes you and Sia meet on the northeast top corner of the hangar so you can get him inside." Mathew whispered and lit his digital wrist watch and they synchronized the twenty minutes, "On my mark, now."

Valerie and Mathew shrunk once again, but this time they went into Diana's breast pocket. Diana dematerialized and sank back down into the ground. Sia cracked open the storage room door and left the room once the coast seemed clear. He slowly closed the door behind him and flew off looking for the security control center and air traffic control tower.

Diana glided slowly through the ground passing foundations, piping, and several unexpected reinforced areas. She would fly her head above ground to peek and see where she was going and what was going on above her every now and then. She arrived to the intended hangar and easily entered. The inside was lit with white ceiling lights. An F-35 lightning II was parked in the center. She saw an office and flew towards it underground in case they had active cameras in the hangar. The room she thought was an office turned out to be a reception office connected to a hallway into other offices. The hangar seemed empty, but this did not comfort her. The lights were off in the offices, but that only meant that people would not be walking around and that if security was as good as expected, there would be motion detectors in the rooms or on the doors. She looked around and didn't spot motion sensors covering the room, but there were security contacts on the doors. More than likely the motion sensors were outside where the plane was parked. Diana checked twice in all the offices. When she was satisfied, she materialized to normal. Valerie and Mathew came out, and grew back to normal size. Mathew scanned the area. 'There are five motion sensors there and there. Two cameras, there.' Mathew pointed them out as he stood next to Diana with her following his finger.

"Okay, I will disable them when you tell me." Diana replied.

'For now, we will wait for Sia.' Mathew signed.

Twenty minutes was soon up and Diana met Kyle outside the hangar. She promptly took him to Mathew and Valerie.

"The tower is five hangars down. They seem to be useless with all their computer systems down. The security center is a make shift TOC (Tactical Operating Center) in a hangar next to the tower. I guess they had to construct an internal communications network and security feed since the virus took out the one already in place." Sia reported.

'Good, Venom after you take Sia outside again, you can disable the sensors and loop the cameras for forty minutes. Sia, I need you to keep an eye out if we are given away. In exactly sixty minutes we can link in the same corner of this hangar except at the base. You can pick up Hummel and me, then you and Venom will go your routes out of here.' Mathew instructed.

"What do you want me to do if you guys get found out prematurely?" Kyle asked.

'You come get Venom and Hummel to safety. I will distract them and get away on my own.' Mathew said knowing that this was a drill they already knew, but it was good that Kyle asked to make sure everyone was on the same sheet of music.

Diana took Kyle outside and returned to the hangar where the camera feed was, creating a video loop. The motion sensors were disabled a few minutes later. In less than forty minutes everyone was in place ready to actually touch the stealth fighter. The loop started, and Kyle saw a very faint flicker on the screens where the security guards monitored, but they didn't see it being so accustomed to seeing motionless aircraft on the screen and a few static disruptions on a rare occasion. Diana entered the office room and Valerie and Mathew flew into her pocket. She flew through the wall and into the open bay landing on top of the fighter. Valerie and Mathew grew back to normal size and started to unpack their back packs. Both packs were full of the specially designed electronic disks identical to the ones they used in Fort Knox. Mathew jumped to one end of the wing and started placing the disks exactly two feet apart. Valerie and Diana took opposite ends doing the same. They used a string two feet long to ensure the intervals were precise covering the plane's surface. Each disk was turned on as they were placed and in less than ten minutes, the entire top surface of the fighter was covered every two foot squared. They continued to cover the sides of the plane, but this time the intervals of the disks extended to five feet, to include underneath the craft. Mathew did a quick check all around the fighter to ensure the disks were activated and properly spaced. Once Mathew gave a thumbs up, Valerie and Mathew stood on top of the fighter. She shrunk along with Mathew and the entire fighter to the size of a half dollar coin. Diana carefully picked the plane up with a metallic scoop and slid it into a metallic box. Mathew and Valerie latched the landing gear anchoring the plane to the foundation of the metal and rubber surface of the box. The movement of the box would cause great shifts of weight even at that size, but Mathew was there to hold on to the front landing gear of the plane. His special ability to increase his density and stay fixed on one location with herculean strength helped to keep the plane from being damaged with movement within the box.

Diana waited for Valerie and Mathew to stabilize and secure the plane in the box, then slowly picked the box up and placed it in a spherical container. The container had a uniquely crafted gyro system so the box would stay centered and upright. It did not guarantee the airplane would not move in the wrong direction, but it helped greatly so that the craft would not be further damaged during the transportation phase.

It was a few minutes later when Diana turned into a ghostly figure and walked through the hangar wall in the rear corner. She sunk into the ground with only her head above ground, waiting for Kyle to arrive. A few minutes passed and Kyle appeared out of nowhere in a kneeling position staring at her head. "Did you miss me?" Kyle joked.

Diana floated up exposing her entire body. "Just show me where to go, little brother."

Kyle pointed towards the bus area half a mile from their location to the southwest. "I got your back." He assured her.

"Okay let's go." Diana said and flew up above the hangar hugging the large high structures and darkness. Her ghostly appearance helped in hiding in the dark and flying at hangar rooftop height kept wandering eyes at ground level from seeing her movement. There were lights around the southern hangars. It was an area of high traffic with many people walking about working at tables and on large flat beds. They carried supplies for disaster relief. Diana came to the top of hangar overlooking the majority of the crowd. Tables and tents were set up. A line of Soldiers and workers prepared boxes of food, medicine, hygiene essentials, and drinkable water. Many boxes were moved into storage in hangar 3, and the rest were loaded on trucks to be shipped out. Diana thought for a moment. The supplies were probably for the workers and families who lived nearby inside the perimeter of Area 51. The Killer Virus had hit the complex late in the game, but it seemed because of it, they were just deciding to act. What a relief because there seemed to be vehicles getting ready to transport things away from the airfield tonight.

"Looks like there is a four truck convoy about to leave." Kyle whispered into Diana's ear.

"I see them." Diana replied to the invisible speaker, and picked her targeted location. She flew around avoiding the lights and got within sixty meters from the last truck which was lined up ready to leave. Her body disappeared into the ground and her head stuck back out of the ground five feet from the truck a minute later. She sunk her head back down and came up underneath the truck. This time she went through the undercarriage of the truck and into the back. It was dark inside, but she found a spot where she could materialize to her normal self.

Kyle grabbed on to the third truck and shortly afterwards the convoy was on its way. Ten miles down the road, to the north the convoy turned towards the west, then north again. A complex of buildings in the distance told Kyle that they were approaching the convoy's destination.

It seemed like a small town in the middle of nowhere. Street lights were out and there was no one on the streets except for several security vehicles. There must have been a curfew in place to maintain order and a safe environment due to the effects of the computer virus. The trucks stopped in the middle of town where a dozen people waited to off load the payloads. Kyle flew to the last vehicle and waited for Diana to pop out through the bottom.

Diana's head came out through the hot underside of the truck. "Go behind that yellow house I will meet you there." Kyle said and scooted himself out from underneath the truck and flew to the backyard of the yellow house.

Diana soon appeared in the shadows of the property materializing to normal. Kyle saw her and touched her shoulder. "It's me."

"Now what?" Diana asked knowing that they were still within the Area 51 perimeter.

"I guess we just fly north until we hit a highway, then go east to our getaway point." Kyle said, knowing that they might trigger possible sensors that were in place between the town and the fence line perimeter of Area 51 owned grounds.

"Okay, let's go." Diana dematerialized again and flew at top speed north staying fifteen feet off the ground.

Kyle flew invisible next to her matching her speed of 160

mph.

They soon sped by a fence line which seemed to be used for cows. It was too close to the town so they kept flying and fifteen minutes later, they past another fence line. This one had posted signs which they cared not to stop and read. Shortly afterwards they came to Extraterrestrial Highway which they bypassed as well and flew about half a mile north then straight east towards highway 318 and Nesbitt Lake.

They came up to their destination two hours before midnight and drove east to route 93 then north for an hour before coming to a secluded area of wilderness. The fighter was returned to normal size, and as quickly as it was normal size Mathew moved away from the fighter and Valerie made herself and the plane small again. This time they were the size of a one foot plastic model plane. Mathew carefully placed the fighter in the back of their Sports Utility Vehicle (SUV) with special tie downs to keep it from moving around and being damaged.

They continued north towards Pocatello, Idaho, for a little less than four hours. The trip was uneventful all the way to a pre-bought warehouse where they off loaded the fighter and left it there for other people to worry about. Mathew and his team got rid of their vehicle in Twin Falls, and took a very restful plane trip to Sacramento, California that morning.

# Chapter Thirteen

# The Truth

T he four international accounts were each filled with $200 million US dollars. It was not the most profitable theft, but to them it was the most satisfying to pull off as a team. The computer Killer Virus was neutralized worldwide by the Eternal Champions shortly after the theft, and things were slowly coming back to normal daily living. They spent two weeks enjoying the luxuries of a millionaire's club resort.

It was on the last day when they received a message to meet Sir Lanhurst that evening at his Sacramento estate. The group was enjoying a game of Dance Dance Revolution, mostly making fun of Kyle and Diana as they fooled around at the highest difficulty settings. Mathew received the encrypted text message on his secure pager. He did not tell the team immediately, but sat there in deep thought. Valerie noticed his changed mood, grabbed his forearm and stared at him waiting for his attention.

Mathew looked at her beautiful face. "We all need to talk." He said.

"Kyle can you pause the game!" Valerie yelled over the music.

The two looked at Valerie disappointed, but her stern face changed their mood to seriousness and they complied quickly.

"Lanhurst wants to meet us at an estate which apparently he has in the Dover district north of here." Mathew said.

Kyle sat next to Mathew while Diana sat across from the three. "It's about time he gives us a proper pat on the back. How long has it been, a year?" Kyle stated, feeling more appreciated.

"What's really bothering you Mat?" Valerie asked.

"Lanhurst giving us a party is nice and all, but think about what we have done. The things we stole in the past were systematic, and they all lead up to this point where we stole a top secret military fighter. Don't you find that odd?" Mathew asked.

"Since when did we care about what we steal?" Diana stated.

"Never, but maybe we should this time." Mathew replied.

"Why the change of heart?" Diana asked seeing that he thought it seriously enough to speak audibly this entire time.

"Do we really know what he is going to do with the fighter?" Mathew asked.

"Probably sell it for parts or if not, to the highest bidder." Kyle surmised.

"And who is that? Australia, Iran, South America?" Mathew questioned.

"South America doesn't need that kind of technology. Australia, maybe; Iran, definitely." Valerie stated.

"That's not the point, technology like that can give a Mid-Eastern country the power to win a war against Israel, or even the capability to assassinate political targets. If Australia needs the technology, it could put them up to par with South America. Who knows what will happen." Mathew stated.

"I don't think that technology even comes close to what South America has, but Mat's right. We never stole things before that could threaten the national security of another country." Diana agreed.

"So why did we?" Kyle asked knowing that Mathew could have pulled the plug on the mission when it was brought up. Ever since Mathew and Valerie were married, the team lived together as a family and everyone trusted Mathew's decisions, so they never questioned the mission; until now, only because Mathew opened up the can of worms.

"Because if we didn't, Lanhurst might have got someone else to do it. He could be selling it back to the US as ransom; but regardless of what he does, we now have a reason to separate from him, even if the fighter goes back to the US."

"Is separating from him a wise thing to do?" Diana asked

with no real concern showing on her face.

"We'll know soon. Ladies and gentleman, our leader's recon starts when we leave for the estate tonight. Diana I need you to look at people and things that relate to David. Kyle I need you to scan for all in and outgoing transmissions. Hopefully, we can get a lead on his network system, and also find out what he did with the fighter. I will analyze the security around him. Valerie, I need you to get as much insight on his personality and intentions. We will need a safe house that not even he knows, so we can track where he goes." Mathew laid things out.

"What if this party is to see where we stand and he decides to get rid of us?" Kyle asked.

Diana looked at Kyle with a prideful smile. "Very good. But I don't think he will be dumb enough to try and kill us."

"No, I was thinking more on a mutual merger slash partnership. He is very business focused and having us as enemies, is suicide for his empire, so he might agree to a full partnership." Mathew stated.

"If that is even a consideration for him, which I doubt; how long do you think that partnership will last?" Valerie asked.

"Not sure, but it will put us in a better position to pull the strings in the long run. We might be able to retrieve the fighter and simply do our own jobs as we see fit." Mathew stated.

Diana grabbed her long red hair with both hands and made a pony tail in the back. "Okay, I guess it's time for a shower and a nice dress, you can give me the mini scanner since they will not see it on my jewelry." Diana said pointing her finger at Kyle as she started to walk to her room.

"Roger Madam." Kyle smiled and went straight for the mini scanner, the size of a pin head, and then his private room to also take a shower.

Mathew stood up and turned off the DDR, then sat back down on the soft silk fabric covered sofa. Valerie laid the length of the sofa with her head on his lap. "Darling, what happens if we have to kill him?"

Mathew ran his fingers through her sleek brown hair. "Then he dies, and we live."

Valerie closed her eyes knowing that her husband was right. Lanhurst was no saint and neither were they, but if she had to choose between another person and her husband, her husband would win every time.

### Sir David Lanhurst Estate, Sacramento, California

Evening came and the team drove to the estate in a brand new custom made Black BMW SUV. The estate was large with twenty visible acres as they passed the main gate. Mathew made a note of the security. It was moderate with a dozen guards out in the open, making their presence known, and the rest were hidden. Several vehicles were in front of the four story mansion, with a few specifically parked for security purposes. If it wasn't for his special senses, Mathew would not have noticed two snipers on the roof, who were very well camouflaged. The US President would have similar security compared to Lanhurst, but that was expected. It really didn't matter too much on how well the security in particular was at the mansion because if Mathew was right, Lanhurst might visit this location only once every few years. According to Kyle's research he conducted in the past, Sir Lanhurst's main home was in New York. Even there, he probably spent only six months out of the year. Lanhurst traveled a lot and had several temporary international residences on top of the many commuter residences in the US. This residence was one of those commuter properties he used to visit his leaders in the region.

The French Gothic architecture features of the mansion were mixed in with modern materials and slight modifications were made to enhance energy conservation and durability. They parked the car a distance away not using the clearly present valet service. There were not too many guests, maybe thirty cars at the most. Everyone kept a close eye on their surroundings, but Mathew was their moving reconnaissance platform. Mathew smelled the parking lot area, noting the different scents of people and fragrances. There was the scent of one weapon, probably a personal side arm. The vehicles were well maintained with almost no leaky scents of fluids. Treads on tires seemed normally worn for luxury vehicles. There were no explosive plastics or liquids sensed with his nose or his sixth sense of danger. There were no pets in the area, at least not from the visitors. German Sheppard's had roamed the grounds about an hour ago but were now either in the back of the property or inside the mansion. Mathew turned his back to the mansion and signed at the team before they walked up to the main entrance. 'Guests seem genuine, but stay alert.'

"Always." Valerie smiled and held her hand up for Mathew to grab.

Mathew grabbed his wife by the hand and turned back around escorting her into the mansion.

The female receptionist was very courteous, and addressed them according to their most recent covers. The entryway also held six security guards dressed like secret service agents. A sign-language interpreter was available, but Mathew declined as Valerie would act as his interpreter. They passed a large arching passageway, but they knew that it was a sonic scanner. It did not beep, but it didn't need to. The security would keep an eye on anyone with weapons, but allow them to carry them if they had permits. Otherwise, the scanner would detect weapons out of the normal or explosives would alert them so they would take care of it discreetly. The team turned over their warm coats and overcoats at the coat room. It was all part of the show because none of them needed warm clothing for the cold weather with their superhuman body makeup.

The mansion had large rooms for entertaining with the main ballroom as the center of attention with large circular tables arranged in clusters and horseshoe shape around a large rectangular table. Sir David Lanhurst was also receiving people as they entered the main room. Less than a hundred quests mingled outside of the main dining room.

The team got their turn and approached David. Valerie walked up as the three stood next to her.

"Mr. and Mrs. Malleson, welcome to my retreat." David

greeted them. His very cleanly trimmed blonde full beard complimented his smile and green eyes. He was in his late sixties, but had the body of an Olympian. He wore a very expensive shiny charcoal three piece suit with a bow tie.

"It is a pleasure to see you again, Sir Lanhurst." Valerie replied with a hand held out after Mathew slightly bowed with a silent greeting.

David kissed the back of her hand, "It is my pleasure to see all four of you." He bowed towards Kyle and Diana. "Mr. Saitou, and Ms. Hammon."

They both bowed, Diana not extending her hand to him. "Feel free to enjoy yourselves, I have a special surprise in store for you after dinner." David smiled and turned to his personal secretary. "Make sure they sit at my table."

The very young blonde nodded. "Yes, Sir." She motioned to the four for them to follow her.

David, waited patiently for more guests to arrive as the team was led to their table. "Your seats are here, you can roam around the mansion, but please return to your seats when the dinner bells ring." The young women instructed touching their seats which already had their name cards placed in front of the chairs.

Their seats were at the large rectangular table which covered a little less than a quarter of the room. Lanhurst was at the head with four people separating him from the team, paired up and facing each other. The other end of the table was empty. The setup of the tables had an open area at the end of the main table for possibly a presentation or show. There were four very large flat screens around the room hung high to cover the room from all seats. The ceiling was very high with very intricate wood beam designs and numerous high hanging miniature crystal chandeliers. The ceiling of the room alone must have cost over a million dollars.

What was really impressive was the list of guests. The team roamed around in pairs. One Congresswoman, the district attorney, four CEOs, several judges, two bank owners, and three movie stars canvassed the scene. Secret service was in the house, but they were only a small part of security. There was no media present -local, national, or paparazzi.

David also roamed the mansion speaking with everyone he could. The charisma he projected was not faked and was well received. It wasn't very long before Mathew spotted Cynthia Bellows, known as Evergreen to the underworld. Her very long almost white flowing hair draped over her exposed shoulders and neck extending to a very elegant but simple pink dress. She noticed Mathew and Valerie looking in her direction, but she simply acknowledged their presence and continued to speak with the people crowding around her.

Mathew and Valerie didn't get much more intelligence on the people and security around them before the bells started to ring. There was a waiter in each lower room of the mansion ringing a four inch silver bell announcing for everyone to gather in the dining room. People streamed into the dining room, Mathew made a quick count of 122 guests, 17 food workers, and 20 plus security personnel inside the mansion. The dinner commenced with a short speech by David welcoming everyone and announcing his opening of two new private schools, and a children's hospital in the Sacramento area. It was received with applauses, as well as the very fine spread of lobster, Alaskan crab, duck, Pheasant, Elk, Mako shark, tenderloin steak, and a diverse vegetarian spread of beans, vegetables, salads, soups, cheese, and breads.

The team did not eat until Mathew took the first bite, even though everyone else had started after the customary toast by the host. Mathew's approval of the food told them that there were no poisons in the food or drinks. It was not his sense of taste or smell that told him it was safe, it was to a point that, but his sixth sense of danger told him, he or anyone else was not in danger. And to Kyle's delight it seemed, because he eat a portion of all the dishes available. Diana was almost embarrassed by his gluttony, but let him have his fun, because the food was wonderfully prepared with her own desire to act like him. None of them needed to eat because of their unique superhuman makeup, but eating for them was more for the pleasure of tasting foods which was why they could soak in tons of sweets, liquor or Carbs, and not gain a pound for months on end. Unlike most of the guests, David ate very healthy choices, which was easy to do on this occasion as the food was prepared with all natural ingredients, nothing was placed in a microwave, and the desserts were very tasty and very low in sugar. He kept to the salads, fish dishes, and a small portion of Pheasant.

Valerie kept an eye on David, and noticed that he was at the time all smiles and laughter, but for some reason was attentive to what the team was doing or perhaps how they were enjoying the night so far. The important people in the mansion may all be working for him, or they were just a cover to for him to be able to see the team in public. But why would he need to be seen in public with them, or want to for that matter? If the team were compromised then it could be linked back to him by association. She wondered what kind of surprise he had in store for them after dinner, but nothing came to mind. Mathew on the other hand had many thoughts running through his head, but most were strategic in nature. He too thought about the possibility that Sir Lanhurst's empire employed thousands of people in very high places. The problem with that was control or lack of control in the organization. If there was a master plan, only one or maybe a handful of people would know who was who and could link things together. Almost like a combined version of a mafia network and terrorist splinter cell type of organization. Whatever the deal, Lanhurst had tight reins on the empire and all seemed to be second nature to him. If someone got out of line, he was sure that they would be eliminated swiftly and quietly as possible.

It was late in the evening when the guests being quite full sat there looking at the highlights of the construction of the new private schools and hospital dedicated to the needy children of Sacramento. It was a very wonderful Thanksgiving for many families the month prior and the presentation was well worth beholding as many smiles and hugs were given to children, teenagers, and families. Generous donations were not requested, but were accepted at the end of the closing remarks.

People were invited to stay and dance into the night. Half of the guests stayed for some dancing. Cynthia was one, who stayed and was always in a corner or by the entrance. It was not long after with less than a dozen people remaining when the personal secretary, Ms. Trend, told Valerie to gather the team for a private conference with Sir Lanhurst.

Everyone was coolheaded and alert even though they drank wine during dinner as they were escorted to the west end of the mansion. Mathew could sense Cynthia following them but kept out of the line of sight. They passed by several rooms and entered two hallways which ended up at a double door leading to the library.

Mathew could smell the books old and new, along with scented cinnamon and oak. He heard a faint crackle which sounded like burning wood in a fireplace. The secretary opened the double doors and closed them after the team entered. David was standing by a clean limestone fireplace mantle. The team was alone with David in the large library which took up three floors and many small windows in the upper section of the massive inventory of books and shelves.

"Please sit." David said motioning to the three sofa chairs facing the fireplace.

Mathew and Valerie sat in the center sofa, while Kyle and Diana sat on their own sofa at opposite ends.

"I don't have many opportunities like this, so I just wanted to tell you how much I appreciate your work." David started. "The surprise I have for each of you is simple. Even though I have been in the shadows, I want someone else to take over my large empire. I have decided to step back and let you four run it. However, there are some stipulations that you cannot break." David paused to see the slight surprise on Kyle's and

Valerie's faces. Mathew and Diana kept a straight face, but they did seem to be very interested.

Mathew signed while Valerie interpreted. 'You have been running the organization for a long time, why the sudden change, and why us?'

David was pacing back and forth during his speech, but he stopped in front of Mathew. "Do you know how many people have failed me in the past?" He paused for a split second.

"Too many. I had some fool working as a bank supervisor try to steal the counterfeit money that was going through the system three months ago. Instead of doing what he knew he should do, like make sure it got into specific accounts, he moved it to a different account. I suppose he thought he would access the account later. But that is not how we do things when I am in charge. His actions almost cost us the insurance transaction of the supposedly stolen counterfeited money, and the authorities could have tracked the money to one of my companies. Now, I know that this particular incident would not have led the police to my door, but it would have started a chain reaction, a reaction where the government or superhero groups would eventually hurt this organization in a very bad way." David explained and continued to pace between them and the fireplace.

"Excuse me Sir, but we don't know all the intricate workings of your fine empire." Kyle simply put it.

Mathew half smiled. 'Sir Lanhurst,'

"Please call me David." David interrupted.

'David, what Kyle is trying to say is that we understand

that there is money laundering being conducted at a massive scale and that stealing is only a part of the organization, but what does an foolish banker have to do with us running your empire?'

David walked to the side and pulled a foot rest a few feet in front of the team and sat. He had taken off his jacket, rolled up his sleeves, and loosened his collar when dancing started on the dance floor, and now he seemed very comfortable as he talked. "Everything I have asked you to do you have done, without questions or complaints. You are experts in staying behind the scenes, and I know you are not cold blooded murderers. I know I can trust you four to take control of this empire and not use it to waste away or harm people. You see, if all I wanted was power or money, I would have checked off my checklist a long time ago. No, I want to enjoy what I have while I still have it, and believe me it's a lot."

"I'm a little confused. What led you to believe that we would want to be in charge?" Diana chimed in.

David smiled and intertwined his fingers in front of him. "We will be in charge, half and half."

'So, if I say we get someone to steal the President's pet dog just for kicks, you will be able to say no and stop operation Eagle Minus One?' Mathew joked.

David almost burst out into laughter. "No, no. It is not like that. If you want to destroy the organization with foolhardy crimes, it will be your down fall - not mine. Once you take over, I will not be blamed, and believe me, I will never see a court room for anything illegal in the past. Now if you tell me what you are doing, I would strongly recommend against it if I think it is stupid. As long as I get to control certain companies and enterprises, you can do what you want with the rest." David explained.

'So are you still going to control the assassins like the one on the other side of the door' Valerie translated for Mathew, almost not wanting to.

David looked at the double doors, then back at Mathew. "You mean Cynthia? No, she will work for you. She is a fixer, not an assassin. Believe me, she knows how to fix things." David said proudly.

'Really?'

"Cynthia, please come inside!" David yelled loud enough for her to hear.

Cynthia entered, closed the door behind her, and casually walked a few feet before stopping, "Yes, Mr. Lanhurst?"

"Come, join us, it is about time you get to know my replacements." David stated.

Cynthia looked intrigued and walked up to Kyle, sitting by his side. "Does this mean I have five bosses now?" Her evenly pitched feminine voice and English accent gave Kyle an enjoyable chill.

"Actually, you have one boss, Mathew." David said and pointed at Mathew.

'I thought we were partners?' Mathew signed while Valerie continued to translate.

"Well you are all equally invested in the organization, but

when it comes to Cynthia, you will have the last say so on anything you want her to do." David explained.

"So how does all this transfer of power happen?" Diana asked.

David sat straight up and placed his hands on his knees. "Well, my lawyers will be getting with you in an hour and all the legal documents will be signed. You will have all day tomorrow to look them over and then each of your will get personal assistants to manage the organization. You can hire or fire anyone you like, but remember many of the people who will work for you are volunteers and are compensated for their loyalty."

"Interesting." Diana replied. "So, how much money and power are we talking about?"

David looked at all five of them with a grin. "Multi-billions for each of you, and leverage in all states and most countries worldwide."

"How much of that is legal?" Kyle interrupted.

"About 97%." David said candidly.

'I see that the organization's illegal activity is just a hobby to you.' Mathew signed.

"Many people can call it that, but to me it has always been business and pleasure at the same time. The power is what I really wanted at the beginning, and now I have it."

Kyle smiled and turned towards Cynthia. "Well that's all nice and all, but since we still have an hour or so, would it be okay if you and I go to the dance floor?"

Cynthia's green eyes slightly widen, being caught by surprise. She tilted her head and smiled. "Sure why not."

Kyle and Cynthia walked out of the library holding hands, while the other four looked on not sure of what to say.

Mathew was the first to break the silence. 'David, I take it you have somewhere we can stay?'

David's face showed disbelief. "Yes, there are three rooms upstairs. Ms. Trend will show you, and if you need anything, she will get it for you."

"Why are you so surprised about Kyle and Cynthia?" Valerie asked, noting his expression.

"Cynthia is sociable, but she is a loner and I have never seen her with anyone as a date. In fact she told me she was going to leave after the meeting. This is the first time I have ever seen her willingly stay." David explained.

"Hmm, and I thought little brother didn't have any real female charm." Diana whispered under her breath.

Mathew smiled having heard her quite clearly. 'Well, I will like to thank you for us and Kyle's absence' Mathew signed, stood up and extended his hand.

David shook Mathew's hand and then the other two ladies, even Diana's hand.

Mathew and Valerie went to the dance floor while Ms. Trend escorted Diana upstairs to her room. David stayed in the library, but soon left the mansion for his next engagement for that morning.

The two couples danced into the late morning. Mathew and Valerie felt different now that they would be in charge. It was weird to them, because it seemed too easy, as if all they had to do was wish for something and it would happen.

Kyle and Cynthia got to know each other a lot more than each of them imagined. They had many things in common and they each had a mutual way of living life. Instead of staying in the mansion, they left together after the legal red tape was taken care of and the dancing was over. Mathew signed the entire night and even in their room. The next day for them started in the afternoon. The three left the mansion and headed straight to a safe house in West Virginia. During their weeklong trip they checked for unwanted surveillance on them and on the SUV. The time allowed them to go over the organization's inner workings as a group. It was a massive empire with no one tied to any single source of wealth or business. David was right, the organization made over a hundred-eighty billion dollars a year in profit, through ownership of over four hundred businesses and private organizations. They had strong influence in all levels of the government, mafia, and law enforcement nationwide, if they didn't control them completely already. The different names and owners of the businesses were all one person. The taxes paid were paid every year without error.

Mathew explained to the two ladies how the organization was like having a nation within a nation, except it had many names. If an echelon of the organization got out of control or was failing, the other businesses would fix it, or if need be someone with special abilities would fix it. The more they read and heard encrypted videos on their laptop, the more they understood many of their own actions in the past. Counterfeited money, forged art, or illegal cargo was stolen or supposedly destroyed in the transportation phase. The insurance would pick up the bill and the company would get compensated in real currency. Stolen money or goods from illegal sources were recovered by owned organizations or special teams. The money or goods would end up in another company's pocket having never made it to a law enforcement office or claims department. Street criminals would think they were pulling off a crime for themselves, but what ended up happening was, they were working for the organization by getting caught by law enforcement owned by the organization. The bank would report $150,000.00 stolen and the police would recover about the same amount or none, but only $100,000 was stolen to begin with, the difference going to owned accounts by the organization. It was now clear why specific safe deposit boxes were taken on their Dallas bank robbery. The money was insured and the bank reported a lot more than what was actually taken since most of it was counterfeit or records were originally and intentionally over inflated. It only worked because the account holders, insurance companies, and bank were directly or indirectly part of the heist.

What impressed all of them was the manner in which key personnel were kept in the know to a certain degree, and how everyone had an accountable part in the organization. It was accountable for each person to do what he or she was told if compensation was desired. The compensation was in the form of under the table high quality medical or dental work, guaranteed employment, high pay, possible upper level advancement, and assistance in personal problems like alcoholism, drug addiction, and the like. The organization started small with two reliable telepaths conducting the recruiting and training of specific people for specific jobs. The telepaths were still employed but only as consultants and recruiting was limited to twenty people or so a year. The organization had a little less than nine hundred supervisors or head people who ran each legal and illegal portion of the businesses. Compared to the size of the empire, there was not really that much illegal activity and they acted more as a sleeping agent waiting to be activated. The laptop they were provided deleted and formatted each specific file that was run, so Mathew made sure they did not go through all of the files so that Kyle would have something to look at, specifically files with his name on them.

They arrived to a large ranch house once inside the state line, and settled in. The day was full of relaxing as they waited for Kyle to join them from wherever he and Cynthia had gone off to. Mathew had a lot of reading material and was very interested in the setup of their positions and companies. He and the ladies were very impressed when they found out that they each had over two billion dollars in cash under their cover names available from several national and international banks. They already owned several properties around the world, with a documented history of over five years. It was ironic now that Mathew had money and power, because it was something he was looking for when he was young, and once he stopped looking for it, it came to him on a gold platter. But in all respects, he understood his fortune was his when he met Valerie and true friends over three years ago.

Things had changed drastically, not because they were in charge, but because they had easier access to David, and the empire. This troubled Mathew, knowing so much about the underground and clandestine operations. Because he was now a person in the public, it made it harder to stay behind the scenes. He and the rest of the group had a permanent address which exposed them to not only criminals, but law enforcement, in particular – superhero groups. There was a slight possibility that Creator or Pandora, would remember him and Valerie's faces because they were now in a public database. The AIs in superhero bases were very efficient, but the only ones that could link them to the Miami truck incident were the Eternal Champions. The probability of them connecting the dots was extremely low, unless they crossed paths for a second time, triggering another and maybe more intense investigation on their identities. Aside from possible issues of this sort, he just didn't like being known all of the sudden. He had been used to starting over with a new life for the third time now, and was used to adapting to the challenges of a family who would sacrifice anything for him. He thought carefully what he would do and how to keep his family safe.

# Chapter Fourteen

# A Guild on a Mission

### 2900 Fuller Street, West Virginia

C hristmas was approaching along with snowflakes as Kyle entered the house's main entrance tracking ice snow onto the floor mat. It was a day after the team had arrived, and things were organized in the house to include the hundreds of electronic devices and parts scattered in the living room.

"I'm home!" Kyle yelled.

Mathew smiled having heard him coming outside twenty meters from the house.

"What happened to your date?" Diana yelled from the kitchen.

Kyle walked through a narrow path past the living room and into the open kitchen family room floor plan. Mathew was sitting at the dining table finishing his desert. Valerie and Diana were half way through putting away the leftovers, but stopped. "You want to eat?" Valerie loudly asked waiting to continue or stop.

"Sure, I'm a little hungry." Kyle replied.

"Okay come here and get it." Diana pointed to the food on the light green quartz countertop, and walked back to the dining table carrying another piece of apple pie.

"Don't mind if I do." Kyle quickly grabbed a plate and served himself.

Valerie stood next to Kyle, "So tell us what happened."

"Well we went to Vancouver, and then Anchorage. We talked and things." Kyle explained as he took his plate full of food to the table.

"She didn't brainwash you, did she?" Diana asked as Kyle sat across the table from her.

Kyle looked at her with a half smirk. "No."

"She probably planted a listening device on him or something." Diana told Mathew and Valerie.

'No, he's clean.' Mathew assured them having already looked for signs of passive and active surveillance on his person.

"So, you just did things for eight days?" Valerie sarcastically questioned.

"You know I thought she was some snobbish cover girl who liked hurting people. But she isn't." Kyle paused for a second. "She is just like me." He proudly stated.

"You mean young, egotistical, lazy, foolish with money, easy to manipulate, slow witted," Diana listed off but was then interrupted by Kyle.

"No, she is caring, goal oriented, very smart, practical, very beautiful, playful and strong." Kyle would have continued but Mathew interrupted this time.

"She is very talented, and all; but you need to come back and get a hold of yourself Kyle. She is an expert in interrogation and manipulation. If you want my help in approving her, you need to forget what she has told you for a little while, okay?"

Diana smiled while Valerie kept a straight face siding with her husband.

"Wow, I didn't expect this." Kyle replied and stopped eating.

"I read her entire file. She might well be the perfect woman, but we need to make sure we can all trust her, not just you." Mathew said, knowing that Kyle was either falling for her or was already there.

"I didn't' expect you to go all crazy on us little brother." Diana added with a smile.

Kyle looked at his friends; they did not have the faces of anger or confusion, but more of concern. "You are just jealous." Kyle told Diana.

"If I were jealous, she would already be dead." Diana countered.

"You got a point there." Kyle unwillingly agreed and

continued to eat.

'First thing is first. What did you find out with the transmissions?' Mathew started the debriefing.

"Well there are several IP addresses that he uses, and I got a few passwords. I think I can figure out where the fighter went to, if I can first find out what companies or teams were used to transport it out of the country." Kyle said.

"Do you think they could have taken it apart to transport it?" Valerie said.

'Maybe, but that would take engineers and more people to do the work. I am guessing whoever it was; they were not US citizens, but foreigners instead.' Mathew stated.

"Hmm, why foreigners?" Valerie asked.

Mathew slid his personal laptop in front of him and the empty plate of pie away from him. 'There are only four other teams that work like we do. This team is used to transport items to other countries. I would use them only because they don't have any ties to the US. If I were a US citizen and see a top secret fighter or nuke being taken out of the country I would be upset about it and might compromise the mission. However, if I was taking another country's technology or treasures out of the country I would just care about the money and not getting caught.' Mathew explained while a list of a 15 person team named Delta showed up on the laptop's 17" screen.

"I take it that they are in black out now until they complete their mission." Diana stated knowing the procedures for the special operations teams in the organization.

'Unfortunately, yes. They are still transporting the fighter, and won't show themselves on the grid until they are done. Since it is taking this long, I am assuming they are taking a ship or ground transport or both to the final destination.' Mathew signed.

"Let me see that list." Kyle asked as he moved next to Mathew to see the screen.

"You know I can try to figure out where they went once they start moving through the airports or train system. That will give us a general idea. Then I can target the surrounding countries for currency transfers. I am sure several companies or a country would pay for the fighter instead of a single private company." Kyle said.

Mathew smiled at Kyle. 'Let's do that, in the meantime, tell me everything you know about Cynthia.'

Kyle nodded and sat back in his chair. "Okay, well, where should I start?"

'Start with you two holding hands in the library.' Mathew suggested.

"Well I'm, going to get some chips and more sweet tea." Valerie said and went off to the kitchen. The team members didn't really need to eat anything. Their superhuman metabolisms completely used whatever energy source they ingested or absorbed. They ate out of taste and not a need to eat to live, or a need to eat healthy choices which normal humans would have to make or face physical consequences for bad eating habits.

The team paid close attention to every word Kyle had to say about Cynthia for several hours. As Mathew had hoped from the file which was now deleted, Cynthia might be an alley they did not expect, but it was a sensitive issue because there was now a relationship in the middle. Things could go wrong very quickly if something bad happened to the relationship between Kyle and Cynthia. The other factor was that even though Kyle said things to indicate that Cynthia had strong feelings for him that did not mean it was true. Kyle could be misreading her and her feelings for him might just be an infatuation.

The team spent all evening talking about the empire which seemed to be under their control. Mathew and Valerie had talked all night together in bed about their future. It was an uncertain one, because they could not decide on what to do with Sir Lanhurst. He knew everything there was to know about the organization, and so far he seemed an upright kind of man by his actions towards them, but all the favorable information they were given might have been fabricated for Lanhurst's benefit. The only way to make sure was to run the organization and the truth would come out in time.

The morning came and they prepped the safe house for future possible use. The plan was set and they each knew their part. They were prepared to start their lives as leaders and not as thieves, with a goal to fight for the right reasons and causes. Not that they were saints now that they had legitimate names and jobs, but that they had a goal and higher motives. Mathew distributed the four cellular phones that came with the laptop and reference material. All the contacts were preprogrammed into the phones. Mathew's phone was specifically modeled for text conversations where a person at one end could talk and Mathew could reply by text, and vise versa. The electronic countermeasures of the house were put on passive monitoring. They left the ranch house and traveled east towards Washington DC.

Diana was going to be in charge of sixty major businesses, to include recruitment of replacement special operations team members. It would take up much of her time, but it gave her access to the other teams which they rarely or never interacted with in the past. Kyle was going to be in charge of eighty companies which included all internet, security, and intelligence focused technologies. This allowed him access to networks and situational awareness of all legal and illegal activity.

Mathew and Valerie would run the remaining two hundred fifty businesses with access to research and development, and most importantly to the social network which supported the legal and illegal activities conducted by the organization. Valerie was amazed at the magnitude of the wealth and power, and she understood that the illegal activities were a very small part. It was an unnecessary part, but as they had stolen for the thrill of it, so did the organization to some degree. It seemed like the organization at this point could not stop without repercussions. They avoided killing people, but they did for various supposedly justified reasons. The truck which Cynthia blew up in Florida also produced unintended collateral damage with the driver. The organization made it right by honoring the insurance from their company, and intentionally fabricating a flaw in the engine produced by a mechanic's incompetence during services. The organization used one of their law firms to sue the maintenance company which they also owned, settling with the grieving widow for 6.2 million dollars. It was their way of legally compensating the family for an illegal cover-up of a theft gone bad. There was also a banker gone rogue who had to be assassinated, but even then the siblings of the single man were compensated through life insurance and a fixed lotto winning.

Mathew texted into his phone and arranged the two assistants to meet them at Baltimore-Washington International airport where they would take the company plane to their new home in New York. He also arranged for Diana to leave for Salt Lake City on her jet, and Kyle would go to Los Angeles that same day. Once Mathew and Valerie were on the plane, they started hard at work coordinating things and gathering information on employees with the help of the assistants. It was in the plane that Mathew arranged for Cynthia to meet him and Valerie at the New York office a few days later. The assistants were very efficient and fluent in many languages to include sign language. What Mathew wanted to know was how much they knew about him and his team. To his relief, all they knew was that they were very wealthy business owners with unique requirements for privacy. They also had the impression that they were with a long time employer which they now saw in person. It was a little odd to Mathew because his and Valerie's names were already in the system for over three years. The majority of the companies were under their current cover names, which meant that David had arranged this transfer of power around the same time Mathew was recruited into the guild.

The orientation to hundreds of people and the corporate environment left Mathew and Valerie constantly busy, but they did take time to speak with Diana and Kyle on a daily basis. Mathew's attention to detail was rewarded as he went through personnel files which David and company leaders did not bother to fully read, in between the lines. Valerie was very good at identifying personality indicators and signs, which she had taught Mathew. He read the files and saw things like a trained talent scout. He had also been around for a long time in the world of terrorism, and this helped in analyzing personnel characteristics and tendencies. He focused on many key leaders and people that would be loyal to him and the group. Loyalty to him worked both ways and he would make sure the people he picked understood that they would be protected and given favor for supporting him always. It was three days later when Cynthia announced her presence to the receptionist of the Avatar Systems Building, owned by Mr. and Mrs. Malleson.

Valerie shortly came out of her office and greeted Cynthia. "Cynthia, how are you doing?"

"I'm doing great Loren." Cynthia smiled and hugged Valerie.

Mathew's assistant opened the door to Mathew's office and announced to Valerie and Cynthia. "Mrs. Malleson, Mrs. Bellows… Mr. Malleson is ready for you."

The two women entered the very modern and spacious office with the assistant closing the double doors giving them their privacy.

"Fredrick says welcome." Valerie interpreted as Mathew walked up to Cynthia offering to shake her hand.

"I didn't know you went by Fredrick all the time?" Cynthia asked wondering why they were using their cover names in a private setting.

"We don't, it's just out of habit." Valerie said, and motioned that they all sit together in the lounge area of the office.

The ceiling was fourteen feet high with symmetric wood and silver framing designs. Two thirds of the office was nothing but one way glass windows. The good portion of Brooklyn down to Governors Island could be seen from the office. The dark hard wood floor, rustic gray furniture, and symmetrically designed light colored area carpet gave the room a peaceful atmosphere.

"But, the office is clean so you can use whatever name you want." Valerie said.

"So, what happened that you called for me?" Cynthia asked while crossing her legs and sitting on one of the two sofas.

'I wanted to talk to you so that we can come to a mutual and lasting understanding.' Mathew signed while Valerie translated.

"Mathew, you don't have to worry about me, I don't want the power and I have plenty of money." Cynthia stated.

'That brings up the question, why were you working for David, and now willing to work or me?' Mathew countered.

"Well, I admit, it was all about the money at first, but now... It's about me. I like fixing things, and I like doing what I want. I helped a woman find her son after a kidnapping one time and David supported me. I have killed people for David, but it was not out of hate or desire to hurt someone. David has helped more people than anyone I know, he is not the cause for drugs in the streets, random killings, rapists or extortion everywhere you turn. I fix things so the organization can continue to help people, not so that the money flows illegally. I assume David had a good reason to give you his empire, so I still work for you because I trust and hope that he didn't pick a bad person." Cynthia explained with relaxed hands on her knees.

'What's the story with you and Kyle?' Mathew changed the subject.

Cynthia hesitated and slightly moved her sitting position. "What does that have to do with my job?"

'Kyle is an owner now, and he is like a brother to me, Val, and Diana. I don't expect a relationship to get in the middle of business, but if for some reason your intentions or actions are deceptive on yours or his part, then it has everything to do with your job.' Mathew signed.

"I am a professional, but if you must know, I like Kyle very much." Cynthia said waiting to see what else Mathew had to say on the subject.

'I am concerned because Kyle seems to be infatuated with you, and if I didn't know any better maybe more than that.' Mathew paused trying to read Cynthia's face. 'I don't want you to give him the wrong impressions and I don't want anyone's feelings hurt. So, I need to ask you when it comes to me being your boss, where do your loyalties lie?'

Cynthia faintly showed a spark in her eye, but kept her cool when Mathew mentioned that Kyle was maybe more than infatuated with her. "I am loyal to you, but I respectfully ask you not to test those limits, because I do have limits."

'If I asked you to go blow up a school full of children, would that hit the limit?' Mathew asked.

"Yes, that would and I would not do it, even if it meant that more people would live." Cynthia coldly added.

'If I told you to never speak with or see Kyle again, would you do it?' Valerie translated.

Cynthia's eyes slightly narrowed and her jaw tighten. "I don't know."

'If I told you to betray David, would you do it?' Mathew continued with what ifs.

"Only if you gave me a very good reason." Cynthia coldly replied.

Mathew's serious face relaxed and he smiled. 'Okay, I need you to have faith in me. I'm not a killer, a greedy person, or an idiot with ideas of grandeur.' Mathew signed and walked up to his very large Mahanoy desk. He picked up some papers and walked back standing in front of Cynthia, giving her the papers.

'I want you to go and report to Kyle. He will give you your assignments. You will shadow him always and fix what needs fixing for him for as long as I say so.' Valerie translated and smiled.

Cynthia glanced at the airline tickets and reserved accommodations for her stay in Los Angeles. "I can get there myself." Cynthia said with a softer and happy tone of voice.

"No, it is on the company. You need to start doing more visible things as a CEO and this is a start." Valerie said.

"Thank you." Cynthia said.

"You will come to find out that business is not all we care about. Have fun." Valerie said as they hugged.

'By the way, did you know that David had us steal a stealth fighter a month ago?' Mathew signed before extending his hand to say goodbye to her.

Cynthia shook Mathew's hand slower once the full meaning of the question was spoken by Valerie. "No, I didn't."

"Don't tell anyone." Valerie commanded, knowing that she would not, even if nothing was said.

"I won't. Thank you both once again." Cynthia left the room with Valerie escorting her outside of the office.

Mathew sat on the sofa looking out into the New York harbor. Valerie returned, bent over and hugged him from behind. "Do you think it will work?" She asked.

"I hope so. Kyle needs someone good in his life, and so does Cynthia." Mathew replied, held her hands with his and kissed her forearm and then her lips.

### Avatar Systems Building Two Weeks Later

Kyle and Diana entered Mathew's office late at night. Mathew and Valerie waited patiently together in the lounge area. The newly decorated office was now prominently light to dark shades of red and black, with white background contrasts. They all wore business attire, which was now a common thing for them to do now that they were working almost six days a week. They greeted each other with smiles and jokes about the décor, but they quickly got down to business.

Kyle had figured out to whom the fighter had most probably been sold to and where it went from there. He did not tell anyone on communication devices, even on encrypted ones, because it was something that needed to be said in person.

"The fighter was transported to Asia. There is a 90% chance that North Korea bought it, and a 10% chance that China has it now." Kyle reported.

"What is up with these chances? Isn't there a way to know for sure?" Diana asked.

"Well the money trail started in Germany, then to China, but ended up in North Korea. The satellite Intel and on the ground sources say it went into China. China doesn't have a facility that can handle the technology anywhere near there. In fact they do have a submarine port several hundred miles north, so if they did keep it, it would have gone there. All this information tells me that the fighter landed in China near North Korea, and from there it was transported to the North Korean border. The transport team that dispersed moved mostly out of China, with a few leaving from South Korea, so my best guess is North Korea." Kyle plainly laid out the logic for his conclusion.

"What do we have on the team?" Mathew asked.

"Most are from Russian background, but there is one Frenchman, a Chinese and three Tai in the mix." Diana said.

"The Russians have access to both countries." Valerie said.

"How much money are we talking about?" Mathew asked Kyle.

"Over six billion."

"That is way over priced." Diana stated.

"Yeah, we got less than 12%." Kyle stated like if they were ripped off for the theft.

Mathew smiled. "It went to the highest bidder, supposedly, but I think maybe it was that price from the start. There was no bidding involved." Mathew surmised.

"Why do you say that?" Diana asked.

"Because, if more countries knew about it, it would be easier to find. No, I think Australia is behind all of this." Mathew theorized.

"IImm... You could be on to something." Kyle agreed. "North Korea doesn't have that much money to spend on one fighter. Even if they did, they don't have the money or resources to do anything substantial with the technology. It is possible that Australia helped them or used them as middlemen."

"Why don't they just take the fighter to Australia if they wanted it so badly?" Valerie countered.

"Because everyone is trying to get up to the same technology South America has. Stealing a fighter from South

America would be almost impossible even for us. But stealing a fighter from the US isn't, and since Australia is surrounded by every intelligence platform known, to include South American platforms, getting a fully operational stealth fighter in one piece into Australia is not going to happen. Unless, they take it to a secure location like North Korea; take it apart and then transport it piece by piece into Australia."

"But why do they need that technology, don't they have it already?" Diana interjected.

"I don't think they do. What I know that they do have is a very large population of superhumans. The aerial encounters where Australian planes were used didn't show any major advantage like the planes South America used in the Caribbean War. It is just rumored that they have a high technology because they were able to close off the world from prying eyes a decade ago. The only real advancements seen are in what North Korea has done with their military because of Australia's support to them." Kyle explained.

"Well what do we do now?" Diana asked knowing that going to steal back the fighter in Australia was a very bad idea.

"I don't know, it is only a theory, hopefully the plane will stay in North Korea. We can manage getting it back from there. In the meantime, it would help if we can find superhumans like us that can help in getting it back and other missions we think we should do." Mathew said.

"We need to make sure where the fighter is before we go anywhere." Kyle stated.

"What if it's in Australia?" Valerie asked.

"We might be able to destroy it, but they will have the technology already. We might not be able to undo what we helped in doing." Mathew sadly said.

"What about David?" Diana asked.

"He's not in charge now, but he might be able to confirm the location of the fighter." Mathew stated.

"He won't know the exact location. I suggest we keep him out of it for now." Kyle said.

"Did Cynthia make you smarter?' Diana joked.

"Ha, ha." Kyle replied.

"Now that you mention it. How are things going with you and her?" Valerie asked.

"She's waiting for me in the reception area." Kyle smiled.

"Well if you have some time, we can go out for a movie or something." Mathew suggested.

"That sounds like a good idea." Valerie agreed.

They left the office and assumed their cover names and roles. The night was very revealing for Mathew. Cynthia and Kyle indeed were deep in a relationship, and Cynthia seemed more comfortable with the team now that she had spent a lot time with Kyle and them. Mathew felt better knowing that at least one superhuman was technically already on their side. Diana would be the one to find and recruit any more that best suited their needs, but time was against them. The world was changing quickly, now they might have to deal with other super power countries and from what was going on with rumors about a superhuman internal war, things were definitely uncertain.

## Chapter Fifteen

O❖O

# Destiny is What You Make of It

L ee flew into the Las Vegas area late at night. He was subsonic as he landed in the backyard of one of his property safe houses remotely located near the city limits. The house was vacant with very little furniture and desperately needed a good cleaning. He took off his armor once inside and plugged it into the wall. It would take several weeks for the armor to recharge, and he would use that time to plan his next move. The armor would charge faster in the sunlight but it didn't matter to him as long as it charged. The majority of the energy used by the armor came from Lee, but it still used energy when not physically touching his skin. It was a year ago since the armor was tested with the help of the SIA, and even though he stole it from them with the help of Joshua, he knew the inner workings of the power enhancer, since it was he who developed it. He thought about finding a lab that had the resources and maybe he would be able to modify the armor so it could be smaller. Maybe something small enough like a belt, being less accessible and conspicuous. It was a stretch because there were only two places in the US with the needed resources and it would not be easy to access them. He also thought about how effective his methods were in crime fighting. It was nice to be able to impersonate law enforcement, but maybe he was looking at it the wrong way. He had been undercover for six months before, but it was limited, because it involved a relationship with a law enforcement person or team. This limited him on where he could go and what he could do.

Lee spent several days settling into the house, cleaning the inside, stocking up on food, and cleaning his garage stored Volvo. He removed the jacks and had to replace the battery, but it was only a slight maintenance issue. The location of the house made it ideal, because the neighbors were not close, and there was no green yard to maintain, so there was no one moving around the house for unnecessary maintenance or an HOA inspecting his property. He spent a few days on the computer catching up on movies and doing research on unsolved crimes involving major thefts, blackmail, and corporate fraud. He avoided murders, drug trafficking, and extortion being that if he was going to go into the underworld, he didn't want to be placed in a position where he might end up killing or hurting an innocent person. Nothing in particular peaked his interest, even the stainless steel hawk thefts; however, being a thief or private investigator did.

Being a private investigator implied that it might be possible that he worked for the right price, and being a thief implied that money was also a defining factor in his character and actions. As a thief he would have access to the bad crowd, and as an investigator he would have access to people in need. After more research he looked at being a mercenary for hire with thieving skills. It would not get the initial results he wanted but in time it would, so he decided to make a reputation for himself and beef up his resume. He would win shooting completions and work in making contacts as a security consultant. The documents for his past would be easy to create by asking Joshua, but he would actually have to win professional competitions to legitimize his credentials by word of mouth and trophies. His new name would be Robert Williams.

He asked Joshua to give him the documents and eight various sniper rifles suited for the purpose. The documents included a recent NRA membership with a reservation to the upcoming Huston Texas Long Range Rifle Match, and an ex-military record as a sniper in the US Army. Lee was very proficient in using the rifles and his powers allowed him to win any competition if he so desired. The match was two months away and he would use the time to advertise his consulting business.

Lee didn't want to go and mess around with his armor, so he asked Joshua to change his backpack and laptop into a belt which supported the defensive attributes; a silver chain necklace supporting his electronic warfare attributes; a watch and a bracelet supporting his weapons; and a pair of Remington glasses supporting his optics. To his surprise Joshua granted the request instantly, with the armor transforming into five separate components. It took Lee a few days to figure out the armor dynamics and improvements over his laptop and backpack configuration. It was more discrete to wear and unless he was stripped naked while a prisoner, there was no reason why he would be completely separated from his armor even if unconscious.

The consulting business didn't get much headway with only a few contacts that would let him know if something came up with possible clients. He looked over his background information which Joshua had created for him and when it came time for the competition he drove to Texas the week prior. He practiced on surrounding ranges making sure he got his timing down along with the use of his optics and scopes. It was very impressive to see Lee shoot without a spotter. His optics ignored the scope and followed the round to its impact location. The adjustments he made were conducted in his optics, but he also physically adjusted the scope on his rifle as well to keep from drawing suspicion to his uncanny perfect shooting. Competition day came and went with Lee winning first place. His standing as an amateur shifted drastically over the next six months as he toured across the USA in Tennessee, Georgia, Arizona, and Colorado. The consulting business didn't pan out even though he had a recent sharp shooter reputation, so he ditched it and concentrated on letting everyone know he was the best shooter in the world. He went international to Sweden and the United Kingdom, but once the computer Killer Virus hit the global scene, he decided to postpone the UK match, and set his sights on going back to Las Vegas.

The Eternal Champions had averted a financial disaster with the destruction of the computer virus, but there were still many people feeling the pains of lost money and digital records. Cindy had kept him informed of her life through email. It was nice to know that she had found a steady boyfriend, a stable life in Seattle, and somehow worked for the Eternal Champions on an on call basis. He recalled Joshua always saying that destiny was what you make it. He decided to move to Huston and shoot for fun at Bayou Rifles where his career had started. He changed things up with a plan. He ensured his credit history was horrible and all his past income was depleted through bad gambling and investments like his consulting business. He picked up a job as an instructor, but it was more so he could get to know locals which he hoped would link him to someone in the underworld. He made it known to everyone he came across that he was looking for a higher paying job and anyone who could out shoot him. In retrospect he was challenged many times, but no one could out shoot him, before or after his return from Europe. Many months passed as routine, and things started to go slightly wrong, He intentionally won second place in a few competitions so that his fame would not draw money he didn't feel like wasting away. It had almost been a year since he started competing, when he received a phone call from a woman who wanted to talk to him about a job prospect with seven figures.

Lee and Joshua had created a very messy history of bad credit and unemployment. He was in jeopardy of being evicted from his apartment in Houston, but it was all real and fake at the same time. He knew that he could move into a place with one room, but the fact that his current and visible financial standing was very bad made him a target for manipulation, especially if there was a skill which very few people had. He hoped it was not a governmental agency wanting him, otherwise he had gone through the trouble of going into ten months of debt for nothing. But he knew that most governmental agencies would not hire someone who was in heavy debt simply because he would be a security risk.

Fortunately for Lee, it was a private corporation which wanted his services. He agreed to meet this person, and went to an interview screening office the following day. He wore used slacks, shirt and tie; but made it a point to look the part of a person in need of financial salvation. It was early in the morning as Lee entered the leased office room of a business building, where a large line of applicants sat. The corporation was named, Tanner Survival Enterprises, and seemed to be looking for survivalists or hunters for a wild game expedition. Half of the applicants wore casual clothes or hunting attire as if they were going to start work right after the interview. Once interviewed, the applicant was never seen, but Lee could see with his optics that they had another exit where the applicants were let out. Out of thirty nine interviews, he only saw one applicant get escorted to another room where he was given papers to fill out.

Lee's turn came up and he entered the interview room where two people sat at a table. A male and a female, both in their mid to late thirties were dressed like lawyers in a court room day view. They had files on the floor and table. Lee noticed that the files were very large and his was in front of the African-American man who read while the woman with a slight Irish accent asked questions.

"Good morning, Mr. Williams. I'm Mrs. Felona Rose and this is Mr. Kevin Moses." Felona introduced both of them.

"Good morning." Lee replied, shaking their hands and sat down in the chair provided six feet from the table.

"I will ask you a series of questions, and if you meet the criteria we're looking for, you will be given legal documents to fill out and then you can decide to continue with the selection process. I will start by asking you what your thoughts are on law enforcement and gun control."

It was an innocent question, but if answered wrong he would not be selected. "I'm not sure what you mean by law enforcement, but I am assuming the police or FBI, so I will say I am not fond of them. They do a job which is not appreciated, and have many problems which I would not want to be a part of. As for gun control, it shouldn't be limited to those people who know what they are doing and are responsible."

"So you mean someone should have the right to buy a gun, and have no problems for several years and all of the sudden they find out their partner is cheating on them and they go kill that person, so is that okay if they were of a sound mind when they got the gun?"

"Well, yes it is. If the man or woman wanted to kill the other person they could have used a knife, a car, or a hammer. If people are sold a gun and they were unstable to begin with, then it is the seller's fault or the bad regulations that gave them access to the weapon. But if some fool wants to use a gun because they are just foolish, then let's outlaw hammers and cars while we're at it." Lee stated with a straight face.

The man stared at Lee with interest but kept quiet.

"What do you think about superhumans doing their own thing and getting away with killing innocent people?" Felona asked, referring to superheroes and collateral damage of innocent people in the news and some in the court system.

"If you are referring to superheroes not going to court or being acquitted of crimes because they were performing their duty as private citizens and in most cases appointed law enforcement officials under the Superhuman Act of 2007, then I am confident to say I don't fully like how superhumans take matters into their own hands, but I think if they didn't then the bad superhumans would have a field day with us normal people."

Felona looked at a piece of paper Kevin slid in front of her. "It says here you have a criminal record, grand theft auto."

Lee smiled inside knowing that the only cars he had ever stolen were in the game, Grand Theft Auto, and that the background Joshua created put him right in the spot he wanted. The background check they had conducted took extensive resources within the prison system to include juvenile hall, and that it would not come up on a police check since it was expunged. It would only come up from a file compiled by criminals, criminals with better resources than the mafia.

"You guys keep good records, but what does that have to do with anything since it was when I was a minor?" Lee rebutted.

"And the slap on the wrist Article 15 while in the Army?" Felona asked placing her fist under her chin as she rested her elbow on the arm of her chair.

"No one is perfect." Lee slightly grinned as if trying to laugh it off.

Felona continued the interview, running down a list of questions which seemed very similar to a personality exam mixed in with control questions according to Lee's documented historical information.

Close to the end of the interview, Kevin asked a question. The question Lee was waiting for.

"If you are hired by us, there will be things which you will be purview to and highly sensitive, of which can legally send you to prison for the rest of your life if you misuse your skills or the information this company has access to. Any incompetence on your part can also place this company in financial and legal dilemma. Having said that, why do you think we should take the risk in hiring you?"

Lee peered into Kevin's eyes. "Short of killing the President of the United States, women and children, or raping someone, you have my loyalty."

Kevin glanced at Felona who likewise looked at him. "You have passed the first phase of this screening process Mr. Williams." Kevin and Felona smiled, stood up and walked around the table to congratulate Lee.

Lee smiled and shook their hands, then was instructed to follow the hallway down to door C2 and wait for further instructions. Lee casually went to the designated room where he found the one accepted applicant waiting in a seat with all of his documents completed. A young woman entered the room and handed Lee a packet of papers and a pen. She instructed him to read it carefully, fill out the requested information, and sign the marked documents.

Lee took the packet and went through it while the other applicant who seemed like a portrayal of a middle aged Soldier of fortune magazine, was escorted out of the room and down the hallway. The documents were legal releases for information, a living will, and affidavit to release the company from any liability incurred by the screening methods or practices of the corporation. It was all legal jargon which basically kept the company from being blamed for any death or injury to him associated with the job. The job description was rather vague, except that it dealt with security using sniper skills and a lot of money. The young legal clerk returned and escorted him to another office where two lawyers witnessed and notarized the documents. He was instructed that the next phase of his screening was conducted at a training facility in New Mexico. He would not have any time to settle anything where he lived and must leave with them immediately, otherwise the screening process stopped there. Lee and the other applicant, who had no problems leaving without notice, were driven to the airport and flown in a G5 Learjet to New Mexico. The accommodations were first class to include the opportunity for them to choose their preferences of sniper weapons, and their own military style desert fatigues and boots. Once they arrived at New Mexico and a desert facility not on the map, their two choices of weapons were waiting for them in sniper cases. The facility was nothing more than a very well maintained newly constructed long range sniping range. Lee could see the security which was moderate, but by the looks of the equipment and lack of many buildings, there was not much to guard. It was more so that lost hikers couldn't just walk up on the range and get accidentally shot. Lee scanned the area and could see a small classroom, living quarters, and kitchen bunker type area, mess tent, range tower, and storage building. He and Henry Ferguson, his competition, seemed to be the only two people there for the screening phase. All the other people were guards, one instructor, a medic, a cook, and one female. He couldn't tell why the female was there, but she stayed in the tower while they were given a tour of their new home for the next three days.

They were in time for dinner promptly served at 19:30 hrs; however, the instructor Mr. Rucker took them straight to the hand to hand pit shortly afterwards.

Lee could see where this was leading, but Henry was an old school Navy SEAL sniper and Mr. Rucker would have his work cut out. Not that he had seen Henry fight, but chances were that he could, if his stories about being in the Navy were true. Henry was in his late thirties, had dark black curly hair, and was in excellent physical condition. He had a small scar on his neck and one between his cheek and left ear. It was either from a knife or a fragment of some kind. Lee was not sure why he got out of the service, but guessed it was a voluntary decision. Now, he either had an occupation he was bored with, or he was in the same situation as Lee with heavy debt and low income employment.

Mr. Rucker was impressive to look at standing over six feet with a very muscular body. He wasn't very handsome, but his rugged complexion showed experience and wisdom. His short hair cut and clean shaven face showed evidence of military life habits. He was not bulky like many muscle bound weightlifters, and had a formidable aspect of strength and agility. He gave his list of martial arts credentials which included Sarit-Sarak and Brazilian Jiu Jitsu Gi, but it didn't faze the two men. Mr. Rucker called for Henry and put a mouth piece in before the fighting started. Henry also put in his mouth piece which Mr. Rucker had given him after leaving the mess tent. He would be the first to show what he knew to Mr. Rucker. The sawdust in the pit was still warm from the hot sun, but was quickly turned up as Henry demonstrated very good reflexes and counter moves as Mr. Rucker defended himself by attacking. It wasn't long before Mr. Rucker and Henry were both tumbling on the sawdust trying to get an advantageous hold on one another. Henry almost got the upper hand on Mr. Rucker, but Rucker was a little faster and seemed to have a little more endurance, placing Henry in an arm lock hold with his legs. Henry patted Mr. Rucker on the leg stopping the bout.

"Do you really want to fight me now; maybe you should rest a day or two?" Lee joked as the two were dusting themselves off.

Mr. Rucker was breathing normally now, and looked at Lee with a little contempt and smirked. "You talk a lot for a youngster." Mr. Rucker motioned Lee to come into the pit and fight him.

"Let's fight!" Lee said and casually walked up to Mr. Rucker almost not taking any fighting stance, and kept his mouth piece in his pocket. Mr. Rucker moved in for the kill, but Lee dodged the two prong hand attack and foot swipe, lifting his own foot out of the way and shifting his entire body next to Mr. Rucker's; countering his hand attacks with lightning speed and hitting Mr. Rucker in the chin with his open palm in an upward motion strong enough to knock him out. In less than half a second, Mr. Rucker was on his back. Lee's speed was uncanny and defied all physics as he had moved a few feet without using his legs or feet. To Lee, it was him moving at moderate speed even without his armor fully activated. A guard approached the three yelling for the medic.

"Mortal Kombat!" Lee yelled with a wide opened mouth then grin as he rotated around, and raised his arms and fists high above his head taking in the ovation of a non-existent crowd of cheers.

Henry and the guard looked at him as if he were crazy or really was a bad ass, it really didn't matter to Lee; his real audience was in the tower. The woman in the tower never left there, she even had food brought up to her and the security film on the windows didn't allow Lee to see colors or other details for identification. He would have to have his optics fully activated if he wanted to see her while she was in the tower; but no matter, in time she would come out to him. Mr. Rucker was woken up by the medic and was given pain medicine for the sore jaw. Other than that, the day was over, and they were told to get some sleep because first rounds down range would be at 06:30 hrs.

The two men slept in a fan cooled open bay room. They talked for almost two hours before sleeping, mainly about how Henry was now divorced and wanted to make money so he could get custody of his daughter and son. It was a messy breakup and Lee thought maybe later he would help the guy out if things didn't work out for him with this corporation. Lee told Henry a little bit about his made up Army sniping history but stuck to the year of competitive shooting which he actually lived through. Henry went to sleep quickly as the lights went out, but before Lee actually closed his eyes, he put on his glasses and his energy helmet appeared on his face. His optics was fully operational for the moment so he looked for the mystery woman. She was sleeping in the tower on a cot and there was a guard near her. Lee could see that she was in her late twenties, about his height of 71 inches, and had natural long red hair. It was bundled up so he didn't know the exact length, but her facial features were beautiful, yet strong. The very expensive jewelry she wore told him that she was very wealthy, but not married. His helmet disappeared and he slept soundly with a tiny smile on the corner of his mouth.

The morning came quickly as the sound of vehicles woke them up. It was 04:43 hrs in the morning, but no one came to get them. Lee could see that three large SUVs with twelve people arrived in front of the tower. They had sniper weapons and complimentary accessories. Lee could make out four sniper teams with the rest as support. They started to set up on the firing lanes but took time to eat snacks in the mess area which was nothing more than a tan colored GP large tent approximately 18 feet wide by 52 feet long. Lee got up and took a shower in the small stall of the restroom attached to the open bay room they were in. Henry also got up and prepped his gear. He waited for Lee to finish for his turn to a shower. The two men went to the mess area with their rifles about 45 minutes before sunrise.

A few men in Marine Corps desert fatigues were in the tent talking about the bad press superhumans were getting and how President Carper was pushing for reforms to the Superhero Group Act of 2000. Lee and Henry ignored them as they got some coffee and a few pastries. "Howdy." One of the men greeted them.

"Hi." Henry replied lifting his Styrofoam cup of coffee.

Lee simply nodded.

"So you two heroes are going to fire against us?" The man innocently asked.

"It seems that way." Henry said as he sat down at an empty table.

"Well good luck." The man said and left the tent, with the other two men following him.

"And I thought we were firing against each other." Lee said as he sat down in front of Henry.

"Who said we're still not?" Henry grinned and ate his donut.

Lee smiled. "Don't take it personal, but I fire against myself and I never miss."

Henry looked at Lee. "You must like stalemates." He

laughed.

Lee smiled mainly because he liked Henry very much. Henry reminded him of Randy even though he was at least four inches shorter; he always had an older mature and humorous aura around him.

The two men finished their snacks. "Let's go show these studs how to shoot straight." Henry said and stood up grabbing his AW50 sniper rifle.

# Chapter Sixteen

# A New Enemy

### Northwestern New Mexico, early December 2010

L
ee and Henry strolled towards the firing line with desert Ghillie suits and their chosen rifles. There were five small mounts fifteen meters apart, each with room for a spotter. The sun was about to rise in twenty minutes or so as they approached Mr. Rucker.

"Welcome gentlemen. As you can tell we have visitors. You two will fire together, one will fire, and the other will spot. You will take directions from the tower through me. Any questions?" Mr. Rucker greeted them.

"Where do we set up?" Henry asked even though he knew the only lane open was three.

"Lane 3." Mr. Rucker replied.

Henry and Lee saw that the other four teams were already in position ready to fire with mainly M42 sniper rifles. Five types of ammunition were stacked neatly behind each firing position.

The two men examined the rounds and looked at each other; there were subsonic and supersonic rounds of various calibers. "You want me to go first?" Lee asked.

"Well if we're going to be a team, I say go for it, Liu Kang."

Lee smiled thinking of his Mortal Kombat episode the night before. "Okay, let's fight!" Lee joked, as he setup his L115 sniper rifle. Lee scanned down range seeing targets set up at 300 up to 2,300 meters. The 2,300 meter target was interesting because it was a shot very few snipers could make with the longest confirmed kill at over a little over 2,800 meters. He could make the shot with ease, but to expect the snipers here to make that shot without many corrections meant they were top of the cream snipers, or the targets were there but were not expected to be used that far out. There were three moving targets within 1,600 meters. The range was setup with a mixture of competition targets and military hard metal targets.

The tower called out to personnel down range, clearing the range and instructed the teams to take positions and fire when ready to the 300, 600, and 900 meter targets. The sun was rising and normally a person would need time to adjust to the shift in illumination, but it didn't matter to Lee. He saw the targets as if they were three feet in front of him. The first round down range was his. It landed high and to the right of the 300 meter target, hitting the outer radius of center bullseye. Lee quickly made the adjustments to his scope as fast as Henry called them out. Lee fired three rounds into the bullseye within the size of a nickel. Lee's optics told him everything he needed to know with distance down to a millimeter, air pressure, rotation of the

Earth, wind speeds, movement speeds, and gravitational pull of the round. He changed targets automatically and fired at the 600 meter target, then the 900 meter target. His magazine was now empty, but three targets had three holes in the bullseyes. Henry looked at the 900 meter target intently. "Wow that was impressive. I don't remember telling you the wind speed or corrections that far out."

Lee placed his rifle to the side. "Do we get extra points for conserving bullets?"

Mr. Rucker came up to them. "Did you hit all three targets?"

"Yeah, can Henry shoot now?" Lee casually asked as the other teams were still transitioning to the 600 and 900 meter targets.

Mr. Rucker was impressed and surprised at the same time. He nodded approval, called into the tower, cleared Lee's rifle and gave them a thumbs up to switch as fresh targets were brought up. He really didn't need to clear the rifle, but it was practice for safety and to see if the men firing were as professional as expected.

Henry quickly positioned himself and started firing while two teams were still busy trying to hit the 900 meter bullseye.

Lee's optics were beyond any known spotter scope or device. He told Henry the adjustments in accordance with his optics information. Henry adjusted very well to each different range, and to his credit, he fired on the money every time. The two men waited patiently for the other teams to complete their iteration. Two teams were almost perfect just like they were, but if speed were a factor Lee and Henry would have easily won.

The sun was completely out now and the 1,500 and 1,800 meter targets were brought up by the tower. They were instructed to fire ten shots into each target. Once again Henry shot expertly with the help of Lee's uncanny spotter skills. Lee's turn came up and he fired as before, but only needed one adjustment. Henry at one point asked Lee if he even needed a spotter. Lee replied with, "Sure I do, who else can I talk to while I fire?" Henry smiled with humility. Lee was by far the fastest and most accurate sniper he had ever known.

The tower put up the 2,300 meter target after all the teams had completed they iteration of 20 hits.

Lee raised his hand and stood up.

"Is something wrong?" Henry asked.

"No, I want to finish this thing so we can eat breakfast." Lee replied.

Mr. Rucker came up to the two men. "What's wrong Mr. Williams?"

"Do we really have to fire all morning to find out we are the best team?" Lee asked.

Mr. Rucker looked at him and Henry. "You really think you're that good?"

"No, I know it. Put up all the targets for lanes 2 and 4. Including the moving targets. And I will hit them all with one round each, using the .50 Cal Wildman has there." Lee pointed at the guy on Lane 4 with a .50 Cal Sniper rifle.

Mr. Rucker looked at the tower and spoke on his radio headset. There was a moment of silence as the teams on the outer lanes didn't know what was going on.

Mr. Rucker received instructions and walked up to the team on Lane 4. He briefly spoke to the sniper, picked up the .50 Cal and brought it to Lee's position.

"You know that the .50 Cal is not as accurate as our weapons, right." Henry whispered into Lee's ear.

"That's why I'm using it to prove a point." Lee whispered back.

All targets were brought down, and then only targets for Lanes 2 and 4 were brought up.

Henry just sat there wondering what Lee was up to. Lee got nineteen .50 Cal supersonic rounds and loaded them in two magazines. "I am using this rifle because it is not the most accurate, but it is easier to fire and faster for my taste." I will fire one round to make my adjustments. After that, just be ready to be amazed." Lee smiled and quickly got in the prone, loaded a magazine, and set the other magazine on the ground ready for reloading.

Lee targeted the 2,300 target in Lane 2 and fired. The round missed bullseye by 7.2734 feet to the right and was high by 3.7862 feet according to his optics. Lee made the adjustments to the scope on the rifle going through the routine, not really needing to from the start. As long as his body was touching the rifle, his optics would make automatic adjustments in relation to the rifle movement, his movement, bore alignment, round, and all environmental factors. All the men on the line watched Lee as he fired the rifle as if in automatic mode, pausing half a second between shots. The rounds left the barrel too slow for Lee, but he was limited by the speed of the gun and its physical limitations. The 2,300 meter target was the first to go down, and then the rest of the targets in Lane 2, the moving targets sounded with a metallic ding as the round hit its metallic center of mass. The front of the mount was watered and built up so that dust would not pop up and interfere with targeting, but as the fifth round left the muzzle, dust was everywhere in front of Lee. The loud bangs could be heard miles away. All nine targets were hit dead center in less than five seconds. It took Lee almost three seconds to reload, and just as quickly as he had put down the targets in Lane 2, the targets in Lane 4 randomly were down. Lee cleared the rifle, stood up and grabbed his own rifle. "Can we eat breakfast now, I'm hungry?"

Mr. Rucker and everyone else stared at Lee in complete awe. Lee walked past him towards the mess tent.

"I taught him everything I know." Henry told Mr. Rucker, following Lee with a wide grin and his own rifle.

Mr. Rucker got instructions from the tower and told the teams to pick up their gear and head back to the airfield.

Lee didn't glance back hearing the commands Mr. Rucker gave, instead he looked at the tower with the corner of his eye. He hoped he didn't over do it, but knowing that there were many superhumans coming out of the woodwork and him being a perfect shot was not too inconceivable. The woman was in the tower talking to someone on a phone, so that was a good sign.

Lee entered the tent and went directly to the mobile kitchen grill. A full breakfast was not ready, but the cook was happy to hear that Lee was starving for his best omelet.

Henry and Lee ate their food undisturbed, even when some of the teams came by to pick up breakfast to go. The teams left within thirty minutes and the woman Lee was expecting came into the tent, followed by Mr. Rucker. Henry's mouth dropped as he saw Diana approach Lee from behind.

"I hope she's a sniper." Henry said almost drooling.

Lee looked at him, then turned in his seat to face Diana up close. Lee couldn't believe how much more gorgeous she looked in person. Her long red hair was not in a bundle now and it extended down to an inch or two above her waistline. Her green eyes sparkled in the morning light along with her red lips which seemed not to be colored with lip stick. Her well endowed and defined figure was astounding to behold. "You must be range control." Lee smiled as if trying to make a pass at her.

"I'm Vicky Hammon, your boss." Diana plainly said and sat at the end of the rectangular table between the two men. Mr. Rucker didn't sit, but with crossed arms, leaned on an adjacent table ledge next to them.

"Does this mean we're hired?" Lee asked.

Diana looked at Henry, then at Lee. "Well it is conditional employment, depending on whether you have problems with stealing things or shooting someone."

"It's kind of hard to steal things with our skills." Lee countered.

"You will be our eyes and ears, plus fire support if need be. We will do the stealing."

"How much is this going to pay?" Henry asked.

"Enough for early retirement and two children." Diana said.

"Has anyone ever told you that you are a goddess?" Lee asked out of the blue.

"They are all dead or fired." Diana coldly replied.

"Well, I didn't tell you, so when do we start work?" Lee blew off her cold reply.

"Ah, he really meant angel." Henry corrected him.

Diana looked at the two men, stood up, and turned towards the exit door, slightly smiling as she left the tent. "Get your stuff, we leave in fifteen minutes."

Mr. Rucker placed a hand on Lee's shoulder. "Good job youngster." And walked out of the tent telling the cook to pack up.

Henry tapped on Lee's arm. "Did you know she was here?"

"I knew there was a woman in the tower, but I didn't know she was a movie star, centerfold, super model!" Lee exclaimed.

"Thank you." Henry solemnly said.

"Thank me for what?" Lee replied.

"If it was me against you, I would have lost. But you took everyone out of the picture, and I got hired because of you."

"You hit your targets and deserve a chance to make things right with your children." Lee stated and started to get his stuff and leave the tent.

"Like I said, Thanks." Henry said, put on his boonie hat and grabbed the last white powder glazed donut from the table as he left the tent with Lee.

Twelve minutes later Lee and Henry were in a SUV as passengers with Diana in the front. Henry and Lee talked about sports, video games, and world news. Diana kept out of the conversation, but every now and then Henry would pull her into a short discussion about who was right, either him or Lee. Diana made sure she was partial and was 50/50 on who won, even though she really didn't agree with either one some of the times. Lee didn't want to force Diana to talk, but he liked when Henry did make her turn her head to the back giving him a chance to see her face straight on.

They once again boarded a private jet two hours later. Lee and Henry were given a change of clothes, and all debts were paid online with some help from Diana's personal law team onboard. They were given fake identifies, very real passports and international driver's licenses for Hungary. They left their weapons on the plane and transferred to an international flight at BWI. Lee and Henry felt like millionaire undercover spies as part of Diana's entourage, First Class all the way to Budapest. Lee and Henry talked about many subjects. Henry was very impressed by Lee's knowledge of legal matters. Lee was very young for his age, but when he explained police and courtroom procedures, Henry asked about what he could do for his martial situation. It was a fragile subject but it became easier the more Henry explained how his wife was the source of all evil. Lee of course knew Henry was exaggerating, and it didn't look all that good for the woman, but it seemed no matter how much he hated his wife, he would in the end do good for her and the kids. Lee remembered all the details and gave Henry options on what to do once his financial situation was completely fixed. Henry appreciated the information and care which Lee gave him. It was a time to remember as Lee and Henry continued to talk about books, movies, people and even anime. Diana was in the same section, but pretended to ignore them as she listened to her music and read on her laptop. Lee knew better, she was always attentive to her surroundings and her position a few seats behind them gave her good over watch on their conversations and actions.

None of the people in the group actually used their real names or normal cover names. It was as if they were all living a spy movie script traveling to another country. Once in Hungary, they took a day to shop for clothes and adjust to the jet lag. Diana was not with them during that time, as they were escorted around town by two translators. A few days of enjoying the attractions ended with the two meeting with their team in a secluded warehouse.

The team they were with had ten personnel; Diana, known to them as Vicky, was the only one on the team they knew. There was another woman, and six other men. Four of the men seemed like locals, or at least acted like it. There were two jeeps and two trucks marshaled occupying a third of the space in the warehouse. They all gathered around a large rectangular table as Diana explained the mission.

"We can get to know each other better as the week goes on. I am in charge, my name is Venom. Hawk here is second in command." Diana pointed at Mathew. "He is a mute, but can speak using his electronic vocal amplifier. Liu Kang here is sniper team leader, *referring to Lee*; Johnny Cage, *referring to Henry*, is his backup." Diana slightly smiled at Lee and Henry. "Speed and Hot Wheels are our primary drivers, *referring to the other woman as Hot Wheels, and a slim young African American man as Speed.* The rest as most of you already know are here for the extraction phase and support for the rehearsal. In two hours we will leave here and start phase one traveling to Romania. There, we will rehearse our theft of a highly classified shipment of space technology via ground transport. The location and detailed description of the real shipment will not be known until a day prior after the 16$^{th}$ of this month, but we do know it will be near the Ukraine border."

"What do we do with our gear?" A heavy set but tall man interrupted.

"You will not take any gear, except the climbing gear already in the vehicles in case we are asked what we are doing driving around. The things you need will be at the rehearsal site and are already across the Ukraine border for the real thing." Diana answered, but her face showed a stretch of annoyance.

Diana continued to brief the group with details and timelines up to the rehearsals without being interrupted. Minor logistical details were fixed once her brief was over. Lee and Henry split up and rode in the jeeps. They entered the Romanian border without incident and traveled slowly for several hours to the middle of nowhere.

They arrived to what seemed a dead end, but they continued off road into the snow covered wilderness. They came to a large valley and a camouflaged row of tents. There was also a large truck a little smaller and shorter than an eighteen wheeler, which was also camouflaged, more against aerial surveillance than from the ground. Lee could see with his optics that a two lane road was flatten underneath the snow and ice for about four miles long. It was primarily straight, but it looped back around to create a figure D footprint. There were two other vacant vehicles parked behind the large truck. Lee didn't see anyone around and concluded that this was a cache and rehearsal site all in one.

Lee and Henry were given a pre-designated tent. The tent held all of their equipment to include ammunition, two cots, a light and heater. They each had a modified .50 Cal sniper rifle and DPMS Panther 308. The ammunition was armor piercing and supersonic which meant that being undetected after the first shot didn't matter for their purpose. If they had to shoot, then the mission was at a high risk of failing, so they were the last line of defense, sort of speaking. They had high tech communication systems with encrypted headsets, thermo sights, and an EW disrupter, used to jam outgoing transmissions. There were two sets of Ghillie suits with snow, night fighter and woodland camo configurations. It was past noon, and they had a schedule to keep.

The group ate C-Rations in their separate tents, and prepared for the first rehearsal of the day. The snow was about a foot deep, and a forecast for another six inches was due by midnight.

The plan was simple; the large truck was the target. It was expected to be moving at 70-90 km/h, and the extraction team was suppose to get inside and take a satellite part, transfer it to one of their vehicle, then allow the truck to continue without the occupants knowing they were robbed. His sniper support position would only allow for maybe one to two minutes of coverage, unless he was on the move. Venom was the lead on getting inside and replacing the part with a fake one. Hawk was overseer on the back of the truck to ensure things did not get out of hand. He was also leader of the on sight security force if for some reason the truck was stopped or law enforcement forced them to stop the truck or their own vehicles. Venom confirmed Lee's conclusion about the mobile sniping position. It would be a fixed position at the start, but they would need to move by jeep to a second covering position once the vehicle made the turn on the D footprint. Once the transfer was complete they were suppose to leave on their jeep. Speed was driving for Lee and Henry, while Hot Wheels drove the distraction vehicle.

Lee and Henry wore their snow Ghillie suits and loaded their weapons in the jeep used for the snipers. Venom, and a team of two men rode on a small truck. One man drove the large truck while another passenger was there to evaluate the drill from the truck driver's perspective. Hawk drove a jeep behind the small truck, and Hot Wheels drove a small shipping truck. Lee and Henry were given a targeted location for Hot Wheels to cut off the large truck causing it to focus its attention to the front and not the back. Lee and Henry picked a spot 1,800 meters away. The jeep was kept in the back making sure it was only ten seconds away, but this didn't work. The jeep was not out of sight so Speed would get out of sight and drive up when Lee called for him. The communication setup was exceptional, with everyone linked into one channel; they could switch to their team channel, and an emergency channel at will. Lee and Henry called out the situation on the ground and the air. Everyone was in position, and the large truck was placed into motion. Everyone reacted in unison, as Lee called off speeds and distances with perfect accuracy. Henry was tracking the area for surprises backing up anything Lee missed and confirming what Lee didn't miss. Hawk was impressed as he heard the reports. However, not everything went smoothly as Diana was able to get inside the truck, but it took too long for the satellite part to be found and replaced. Lee knew that the part was a mock up, but it was still the right size and weight. He saw that Diana didn't unlock the back of the truck or open the door, but instead passed through it like if she was a ghost or something. He saw her move through the truck, but got confused as to her exact location which is what caused them to run out of time. The movement to the second position went well. Lee never had a problem with setting up in the second position, and could have provided cover by himself from the jeep the entire time, even on the move, but he was sure to raise an eye brow if he did that, not that his shooting at the range hadn't already done so; but this was a different group of spectators except for Diana.

The second try turned out with similar results. They could do it within three minutes, but that meant that there was more of a chance for other vehicles or security to see them in the act, and sniper coverage was sacrificed at the end of the stretch. It was almost dinner time and the snow started to come down heavy. They rallied on the tents and ate a hot meal. Lee thought about everything carefully, especially that Vicky was probably a superhuman, and after eating he asked her if he could talk to her in private. Diana agreed and they went to the tent occupied by her and Hot Wheels.

Diana went in first and sat down on her cot. "What did you want to talk about Mr. Williams."

"Please call me Robert." Lee requested.

Diana looked into his eyes. "Okay. Robert, what is it?"

"Please give me the benefit of the doubt, but what if I told you I could guide you while inside the truck so you can find the satellite part in time?" Lee suggested.

Diana's eyes closed slightly. "And how are you going to do that?"

"I will need you to switch to my channel once you get inside. I will talk you through to your target. Only I, Henry and Speed will know what is going on. Once you get it, you can switch back to the open channel." Lee said.

"So you're telling me you can see inside the truck?"

"Just trust me, we can talk more about this later, but the next time you get inside the truck just change to my channel." Lee said and walked outside leaving Diana alone.

Lee thought Vicky was going to go after him, but she stayed in the tent for several minutes.

The snow had let up and it was dark with the overcast and

late hour, but they wanted to get some improvement done.

Vicky was speaking to Hawk before they left to their positions, and normally Lee would be able to ease drop and hear the conversation, but they were signing and he didn't know sign language. It was obvious that she and Hawk didn't keep secrets, so chances were that Hawk knew about what he proposed to her in the tent.

Lee and Henry maintained their selected positions, but this time they would not leave the jeep once they left firing position one. Lee also instructed the two men not to interfere with his conversation with Venom once she was in the truck. They had no clue to what or why he was commanding them to do, but they agreed.

The third attempt started without a hitch. Venom came on the channel and Lee expertly guided her to the part. It took less than five seconds for her to get to the part, which was randomly positioned by Hawk prior to each attempt. The sniper team made it to the second position, but really didn't need to since the vehicles broke contact with ease. The team was happy as they gathered back at the starting point having completed the mission in less than ninety seconds. Lee was riding shotgun when he noticed an energy flux in the distance with his optics. The jeep was a little less than a mile from the rest of the group as Lee commanded Speed to stop the jeep.

The rest of the group was gathering around Hawk. Venom was at the back of the large cargo truck when Hawk took out his side arm and fired into the dark terrain.

"What's going on?" Henry asked.

"Ambush! Four, six, no two things coming your way Hawk!" Lee alerted everyone on the net as his optics saw two objects appearing and disappearing from 800 meters down to 200 meters. Hawk fired his futuristic handgun, which acted more like a cannon as it hit one target in the process of appearing. The sudden and violent impact of the almost invisible rounds from his gun caused the object which Lee could distinguish now that it had stopped moving, being pushed back about twenty feet, was a humanoid android carrying a laser rifle similar to one of his own laser rifle in his armor. Lee's helmet appeared on his head, he scanned the android, but his enray vision could not penetrate the alloy shell of the assailant. It seemed only to slow down a little due to Hawk's weapon, as no physical damage could be determined. He fired his .50 Cal while standing on the jeep, but the recoil didn't push him back into the rear seat. Two rounds hit their targets, one head shot on the farthest target from the group and one head shot on the android which was now twenty feet from Venom. The android closest to the group was able to shoot at full auto with his assault rifle hitting everyone except Hawk who dodged the attack, Hot Wheels who was away from the group and Venom who just stood there but nothing touched her. The other four men died as supersonic laser like rounds tore them up like M2 .50 Cal machinegun impacts.

Hawk fired at the android near him and it was blown backwards taking massive knockback for about twenty meters. The second android was now fifty meters from Venom and Hawk. It shot a red laser beam at Venom, but instead of it going through her like the other attack; Diana reeled in pain as her entire body shook as if being electrocuted.

"Stay here!" Lee yelled and flew out of the jeep with his armor fully activated, towards the two androids, Hawk, and Venom. Lee's sniper rifle fell onto the rear of the jeep, barrel still hot, but cleared and placed on safe.

Henry and Speed looked on as Lee moved silently short of subsonic upon the four individuals having transformed himself into some super armored plated Soldier appearing out of a super advanced single shooter game. The androids were made of an alloy Lee had never seen before, and the .50 Cal armor piercing round or Hawk's handgun was not doing any effective damage. Venom collapsed on the dirty snow as if unconscious, and the android which was attacking Hawk changed targets. Hawk actually took four rounds to his body, but nothing happened to him as they bounced to the side while he stood in position as if he were an immoveable force. Lee targeted both androids, and at max power his two rifles fired a steady laser stream slicing the androids into shreds of metallic scrap as if they were hard boiled eggs in a slicer. His optics sensed an energy spike in one android, which quickly died, but the other android was different. Lee landed next to Diana as Hawk jumped in front of Diana aiming his gun at Lee. "It's me Robert." Lee said out loud and on the coms headset which was not working for Hawk.

Lee scanned the pile of scrapped androids and sensed an unusual energy buildup. Hawk stood between Diana and the scrapped android which was sixty meters away. The alloy of the entire android glowed for a second before exploding into a blinding white light disintegrating or pushing everything around it except Hawk. Lee was thrown against the moving small truck behind him, Diana was tossed fifteen meters along the ground,

Hot Wheels was thrown unconscious into the woods almost hitting her head on a tree. The light didn't blind Lee as his helmet automatically shielded his eyes. There was a crater 30 meters in diameter where the android had blown up. The only working vehicle in the area was the one Henry and Speed were in. Lee recovered quickly from being blown back and flew next to Diana. He scanned her vitals and entire body. She had no broken bones or internal damage to include her skull and brain. However, she did have a few bruises on her arm, hip, and side of the head, probably from debris of the explosion. Hawk's goggles had protected his vision from being blinded. He sensed no more danger so he jumped to where Hot Wheels was at. Henry reported they were temporarily blinded, and would be alright in a minute or two.

Lee scanned the area 360 degrees as far as his optics would allow through dense woods and hilly earth. Things seemed to be clear for fifteen miles all around. The large truck's chassis and cargo was on fire now, which was mainly wooden boxes, plastic and metallic scrap. The other two vehicles were obviously totaled as their tires were flattened or missing a section of their chassis. Lee's lasers had created very long gouge like trenches in the ground where the laser did not make contact with the android bodies. The several trees near ground zero were toppled half way over and snow was cleared being replaced by charred earth. Diana was regaining consciousness as Hawk carried Hot Wheels to Lee's location. Henry and Speed could see now and were racing to their location in the jeep. Lee sat there with Diana, holding her upper body and head in a sitting position with his bent leg.

Diana opened her eyes slowly. Lee's armor disappeared

into his personal accessories. Diana stared into Lee's blue eyes as the reflection of the truck's fire shown on his face and glasses.

"How do you feel, beautiful?" Lee's smile was warm and comforting as his voice.

"Tired." Diana tried to smile but was too weak.

"Hawk can you hold her up? I will check Hot Wheels for injuries." Lee said as Hawk placed Hot Wheels next to Lee and supported Diana's sitting position.

Henry and Speed stopped the jeep short of them, Speed stayed in the vehicle acting as a look out while Henry hopped out to their aid. Henry broke out the medic bag, while Lee's helmet reappeared on his head and he scanned Hot Wheels for injuries.

"She has a fractured arm, two broken fingers, a hairline fracture on one rib, and a large bruise on her rib cage and knee. I will set her bones before she wakes up. Get some morphine ready." Lee said.

Hawk's vocal amplifier was damaged so he signed at Lee, but Lee had no idea what he was saying. "Sorry I don't know sign language."

"He said, carefully move her into the jeep before you set the bones, and get the splints ready." Henry said.

"Why didn't you tell me you knew sign language?" Lee said as one of his laser rifle appeared on his arm, stopping the bleeding on Hot Wheel's forearm.

"You didn't ask." Henry replied as he moved the medic bag to the jeep, and Speed made room in the back by tossing out gear. They used the Ghillie suits to act as a cushion before moving Hot Wheels into the jeep. Lee quickly set her four broken bones and splinted what he and Henry could. Diana was stronger now and was on her feet. The heat from the fire helped her recover faster, but it was also a beacon in the dark night to their location.

"Robert, can you get rid of the mock satellite evidence?" Henry translated for Hawk.

Diana sat in the front while Henry stayed with Hot Wheels. "Yeah." Lee replied.

'We will go to the tents. Meet us there.' Hawk signed.

The jeep took off north straight for the tents two miles away. Lee scanned the entire area again and the concentrated on the mock satellite evidence. He activated his armor and lased all the evidence into molted metal, glass, and plastics. This included the gear thrown out of the jeep still at the scene. He scattered his lasers on the burning debris and surrounding area making sure the entire area burned as if in a forest fire. He then scanned for the second android which was near the first, hoping it was not totally destroyed in the explosion. He found a chunk of android alloy the size of a large stapler. There seemed to be a few more pieces, but he didn't want to take them all or else the creator of the machines would know for sure that they had the foreign material.

Lee quickly flew to the jeep where they had put up the roof to protect the occupants from the winter elements. The tents and camouflage nets were all lit on fire. His armor was white and black camouflaged designed and except for Hawk they were all startled when he landed in front of the jeep.

"Now, can someone tell me what the hell is going on?" Lee asked when he stopped next to the driver side. Speed kept quiet but ready to drive on command.

"Those things seemed to be attacking me and Venom. But I have never seen them before." Diana translated for Mathew this time.

"Who did you guys piss off?" Henry politely yelled from the rear of the jeep while monitoring Hot Wheels' condition.

"What's the satellite equipment for?" Lee asked in another way.

"We can talk about all this on the way out of here." Diana replied.

"I can carry the jeep with all of you in it and fly us out of here." Lee said.

"How fast can you fly?" Diana asked as if flying were a normal thing knowing Lee was definitely a superhuman or a human with super powerful technology.

"Well I can hit mach 4, but the jeep won't last past 200 mph, question is so how fast do you really want to go?" Lee stated as a fact.

"Not that we are in a hurry, but we are, and we need to be back in Budapest within the next five hours, so as fast as you can below radar and without destroying the jeep." Diana translated for Mathew.

"Okay get in, fashion your seatbelts and close the windows." Lee said ready to go underneath the car.

They got ready, and Lee went under the jeep, easily lifting it with his armor and flew northwest towards Budapest. He stayed under the radar down to treetop level flying at an average speed of 160 mph through heavy snowfall, but at times just flew straight as not to give the people in the car negative G-forces. They talked the entire way to the Hungarian border through the working headsets about what could possibly had brought about the attack by those high tech, possibly alien androids. The satellite equipment was needed by the organization to track down the stealth fighter they had procured in the past, but the group was told that it was needed for a special surveillance capability for the US military. Lee suggested that the assassination attempt was to kill Diana and Mathew, not to stop the theft of the satellite equipment. Mathew agreed, upon a second look, and surmised that the androids were capable of killing them, but they did not expect Lee to be there with his special powers and lethality.

Diana told Henry, Hot Wheels, and Speed, that they would be paid $20 million, once they arrived to a safe house in Budapest. They needed to go off the grid for six months, and if they felt that they were being spied on during that time, they would contact her or Mathew on a secure email address. Their families would be taken care of, and that they would be notified at the end of the six months if they needed to change their identities for good.

It all sounded good, but Lee wanted something better for Henry. He was sure that they were not part of the big picture and were simply in the wrong place at the wrong time and would be considered unimportant collateral damage. Lee privately gave Diana a proposition concerning Henry on a separate channel. In turn, Diana told him he would be needed in the corporation instead of lying low, but it was his decision to make. Lee told her, without a second thought, that he would stay with her as long as she wanted.

They landed past the southeastern Hungarian border, and drove almost two hours to Budapest. They dropped off Speed and Hot Wheels at a safe house. Lee and Henry continued to the airport with Mathew and Diana. Henry thought he was suppose to go with Speed, but that was not the case once at the safe house so he played along, having trusted Lee this far with favorable results, so why not a little longer.

Mathew was constantly on his laptop once they got to a cache in the airport. Lee noticed that he was looking for any news of any assassinations past and present with indications of aliens, superhumans, or unique circumstances. Mathew was very proficient in researching details, and it didn't take long for him to see patterns, especially since most of the research had already been conducted by the Eternal Champions. Their information was passed down to the SIA, and now his sources in the SIA told him what he needed. What everyone didn't know was the real names of the people and operations behind the companies which supported the illegal assassination activities, but he knew, since it was his companies that knew about or were associated with the unproven suspicions. In addition it was his team in specific that helped keep Lanhurst's non murdering activities a secret.

## Chapter Seventeen

# Call Me Alpha

### Avatar Systems Building, New York City

Mathew contacted Valerie and coordinated for an emergency meeting and the proposition Lee made to Diana, prior to leaving Budapest. Valerie was having a party as a pretense for Mathew's and Diana's presence in New York. Mathew was going to use that pretense to their advantage, since they were not supposed to be in the United States for real. The four flew back to the United States under completely different names. Once they were in BWI Airport, they bypassed immigration and customs. Mathew and Diana by this time were sure that Lanhurst had something to do with the assassination attempt. There were very few people with the knowledge of his and Diana's whereabouts, and if anything he was in the know when David was in charge, plus the information he got from SIA implicated David by association with the companies in Europe and the United States.

Diana talked to Lee a lot more while in the private plane

heading to New York. After Lee consulted with Joshua in his mind, Lee told her a little about his abilities and that his real name was Lee Frost. This intrigued her because she thought they had very solid intelligence on him, and he seemed to defy the odds with perfectly faked information. Lee didn't tell her about Joshua or his real past, but Diana knew he had many secrets, and in time he might let her know, just like she was keeping her distant past from him as well.

They arrived at JFK airport, and transferred to a helicopter, landing on top of the Avatar Systems Building fifteen minutes later. It was early evening; Valerie, Kyle and Cynthia were waiting for them in Valerie's office. By contrast to Mathew's office, her office was lavishly decorated in various shades of brown, whites, and greens. Her very large desk was tempered clear glass, and furniture was all high grade fabricated leather. The floor plan was similar to Mathew's office, but she had a circular ring of light on the ceiling where everything focused on in the room. The floor was white marble slabs and the palace Persian carpet was the focal point in the lounge area. She too had a very large panoramic span of window scenery, but her view was towards the tall and shorter skyscrapers and buildings of Manhattan instead of the harbor.

Valerie's group knew something important was going to be talked about, but they were not given details since Mathew did not want specific things to go out over the air, even if it was encrypted. The arrival of Mathew's group was also supposed to be a mystery to everyone except Valerie, who made the arrangements in BWI and JFK airports. Kyle and Cynthia were there only at Valerie's beckoning, and they didn't know that

Mathew and Diana were already in the United States, let alone the city.

A team of lawyers were in the conference room along with a security team and a squad of NYPD police officers, one level below Valerie's office. They were working late, but it was on Valerie's orders. Arrangements were being conducted, and time was against them since there was a late evening party at the Malleson mansion which all needed to attend. It was out of the ordinary since only two dozen people where attending two weeks prior to Christmas. Not many people indeed for a billionaire get together, but enough for Mathew's purpose. The information he received while en route to New York, was enough for him to take active measures as leader of the guild. There was an assassination attempt on him and the people he cared about, so nothing was going to keep him from setting things straight in the corporation.

Mathew entered Valerie's office dressed in a black tuxedo without the flare on a white dress shirt, black bow tie, and a long dark gray trench coat, with scarf and dress shoes to match. Diana followed with a long red trench coat, red double-faced shearling hat, ebony black high heel shoes and ebony black silk cocktail dress down to her ankles. Lee walked behind Diana carrying a black trench coat, and wearing a dark gray two piece suit and neutral tie. Henry likewise had a trench coat, but his suit was Duke blue.

Kyle and Cynthia stood up off one of the sofas in the lounge area and walked towards Valerie who was already half way across the office as she met Mathew. She and Cynthia were also dressed for a formal event, Valerie favoring brown and Cynthia white. Kyle smiled as he saw Henry with the blue suit just like the one he was also wearing.

"Darling." Valerie said and kissed Mat on the lips while they hugged.

Diana came up to Valerie and gave her a big hug. "Good seeing you Val."

"Good seeing you too, D." Valerie said as Mathew hugged Cynthia and Kyle.

Diana turned towards Lee and Henry, introducing them to the three. "Valerie, this is Lee and Henry."

"This is Valerie, Cynthia, and Kyle." Diana introduced them by their real informal names.

Lee shook hands with the three as did Henry, Kyle telling Henry nice, referring to his choice of suit when they shook hands.

"Well shall we?" Valerie said motioning everyone to sit in the lounge area.

Mathew told the story as Diana translated for the sake of Lee and Cynthia who didn't know sign language.

Henry knew the story so he was naturally distracted by the wealth and stature of the people in front of him. He thought at first that he was part of a spy movie which included beautiful women, mystery, and danger. But to his relief, it was better than a spy movie, it was for real, and it was better than any military operation he had been a part of in the past. He was in the middle of people who had super powers, money, and a crisis to solve in order to save lives, his and many others like him.

Valerie, Kyle, and even Cynthia were almost in disbelief that Diana almost met her maker at the hands of an unknown machine. A few questions were thrown out there, but all of the strategizing by Mathew were confirmed when the conclusions pointed towards Sir Lanhurst. He would have the answers and if not he would know who to go to and get them. Lee had given the android alloy to Mathew, but that would not be able to tell them much of anything anytime soon without laboratory analysis.

"I'm still a little confused though. Why are we dressed like this if we are going after David, is he coming to the party?" Kyle said.

'No, but my sources tell me he knew about what was supposed to happen in Romania. I need the party to cover our alibis.' Mathew signed. 'But there is also a spy in our mists. We need to convince the spy that we are out of the country, take him out, and then tell the guests what they are suppose to do which is cover our absence. Each guest was selected for their loyalty, except the spy of course. Once David thinks we are not on to him we can catch him by surprise so he won't have time to do anything tricky like order another assassination, take back his empire, alert his companions, or something like that.' Mathew paused for a moment and looked at Lee.

'Lee, can you locate targets from cell phone signatures or land lines?'

"From a cell phone yes, from a land line I probably can, but if it's secure, I will need some time to decipher it." Lee said.

"How much time?" Valerie asked.

"It depends, maybe a few seconds to a few hours."

"I might be able to help with that. I can patch the message into my laptop and cut the time by tenfold." Kyle said being the computer and communications expert.

"So what happens once the spy is neutralized?" Henry jumped in with a question.

"Everyone here except Henry will go pay David a surprise visit." Mathew signed.

"What am I going to be doing during that time?" Henry asked feeling left out of the action.

"I have a special mission for you. I will brief you once we neutralize the spy." Valerie assured him.

"Okay, you guys will mingle with the guests until the spy sends his report to David's people. Once he is neutralized Diana and I will show our faces. Okay Val, I need you to make us all small and Lee will fly us home. Lee, it is important that we get into the master bedroom balcony entrance undetected; we will disperse from there to locations I designate. Any questions?" Mathew signed.

"Do we know where David is now?" Kyle asked.

"Yes, I do." Mathew signed.

"What's the address to your house?" Lee asked.

"1200 Rucker Place, Secaucus." Valerie replied.

Valerie passed out ear pieces with miniature microphones to everyone. Then they moved to the roof. Cynthia flew into the air waiting for Lee, while everyone else gathered around Valerie, except Lee.

Valerie and the people around her shrunk down to the size of an ant. Lee's armor activated and allowed Valerie's group to enter his suit's inside chest pocket. Lee's armor was completely flat black as he flew across the city with Cynthia by his side towards the northwest, his optics leading him.

They arrived at the Malleson mansion balcony with ease and entered the master bedroom. Mathew directed everyone where to go and what to do. Valeria went downstairs to welcome the guests and give a business excuse for Fredrick and Vicky not being there at the moment. Kyle and Cynthia flew outside and approached the mansion main entrance on foot. Lee and Diana flew back outside as well, and took a position in the outer most section at the rear of the grounds in a tree. Lee scanned the entire three story mansion to include the basement and surrounding neighborhood. All was clear as Mathew and Henry waited in the master bedroom for Lee to hopefully intercept the spy's transmission. It was not guaranteed that the spy would report during the party, but Mathew was sure that David would not want to wait to get any kind of report on Mathew's or Diana's whereabouts or health. Valerie was sure to speak to the spy and pretend that something was wrong as if she were anxious. In fact a telephone call was sent to her from her personal assistant that they could not get a hold of Mathew or Diana. It was short of an hour before Lee reported that the spy had moved to a guest room bathroom. Lee picked up an encrypted cellular call lasting twenty two seconds. Diana was there with Kyle's laptop. Lee's armor wirelessly plugged into the laptop, breaking the encryption in less than a minute. The spy was still in the bathroom, apparently using it so as not to bring up suspicion if caught in the room.

The deciphered transmission was played back to all the members.

*Hello.*

*It's me. Mrs. Malleson seems worried that they can't get a hold of Mr. Malleson. Seems like he will not be showing up for real.*

*Understood, stay to the end of the party, I will call you later.*

*Okay, bye.*

"I can take him out right now if you want, but it will put a big hole in your pretty house." Lee stated.

"Shouldn't we capture him and question him?" Henry asked.

"Oh wait. Mathew says No, take him out, we have bigger fish to catch. Diana, you and Lee meet us in the bathroom so we can clean up the mess." Henry said, translating for Mathew.

"Roger." Lee replied and instantly targeted the spy's head firing a laser beam wide as a golf ball passing through the mansion walls, his head and into the bathroom wall.

"Diana, look at your screen." Lee told her. Diana looked down at the laptop screen. She saw what Lee saw in his optics. The entire side of the mansion was as if it was going through an airport x-ray machine. It was very clear and Diana could see the dead spy on the bathroom floor as Lee zoomed in. "By the way, did I ever tell you how beautiful you are?" Lee continued.

Diana realized that he could see through things as if they were transparent. "Have you seen me naked?"

Lee smiled in his helmet. "No, I can't see that way, you look like a skeleton most of the time to me if I look beyond your clothes." Lee lied, being able to see with his optics down to the minute detail. The information gathered by his optics was displayed in accordance with his brain waves, so that it showed him, as he so desired, a virtual two or three dimensional replica of what should be there. This was how he was able to determine colors of her hair, face, and body details when she was in the range tower. But he didn't want her to know that at this point, because he wasn't a peeping Tom and it was an invasion of privacy.

"How come I don't believe you?" Diana said.

"Well you can undress me with your eyes, and we'll call it even." Lee smiled in his helmet and flew off towards the master bedroom.

Diana frowned and flew directly towards the dead spy on the bathroom floor. She was the first one there, flying through the walls. The man's head should have been bleeding all over the floor; there was almost no bleeding, but the stench of burnt hair, blood, flesh and brain matter over powered the bathroom and guest room. Diana wrapped the head with a towel, while Mathew entered and took the phone off his person. Henry made sure no unauthorized person entered the guest room.

Valerie arrived shortly after Diana called for her. Valerie shrunk the man down and Diana took the two outside to dispose of the body. Lee cleaned the bathroom with bleach and sprayed it with air freshener, and then the room was locked from the outside. Mathew, Henry, and Lee went out and mingled with the guests, Kyle and Cynthia staying close to them. Valerie and Diana returned ten minutes later, only they knew where the body had been deeply buried. Valerie made an announcement which was instructions for the guests to say that they were all there in the party the entire time. The twenty three guests were law enforcement officers, prominent doctors, a lawyer and even a district judge. They worked for the organization, and knew that going against the organization, meant signing their own death warrant; but they obeyed out of loyalty, not really having a cause to dislike or fear the organization since murder, extortion or drugs were not part of the organization's practice. Mathew and the group left the mansion through the back door, except for Henry. They went far to the back of the property in the bushes. "Okay, I will shrink you all and Lee will take us to David." Valerie said and whispered the location where David was in Lee's ear.

Lee was soon on his way to Saint-Colomban, Canada at Mach 4. He made a high arch arriving 25 minutes later at a massive estate covering several square miles. The team assembled outside of the estate grounds at normal humanoid size. Lee scanned the massive ranch estate, several buildings and twenty-six personnel. Everyone looked on the laptop as Lee played the information in a stream of video.

"That's him." Valerie pointed at the figure resembling David Lanhurst. He was in the living room watching television, while everyone else seemed to be on alert, patrolling or already asleep. There were no children or elderly; all were adult security personnel which was more than normal for anyone living an undisturbed retired life. The setup seemed as if David were under house arrest or with the witness protection program, only difference was he had twenty more guards than normal. Mathew told Lee and Cynthia to take out the outside security, while Diana took the rest of the group inside. Cynthia flew to the north side of the ranch main building, and Lee took a position on the south side. On Diana's order, Lee and Cynthia systematically killed the outside and worked their way inside. Diana entered the living room and as soon as David saw her ghostly image turn solid, Mathew and Valerie appeared like an inflating car airbag in the same room next to her.

David was startled, "What are you doing?" he said jumping off his recliner sofa.

Mathew grabbed David by the neck with one hand, and held his gun in the other at his side. David tried to take Mathew's steel like grip off his neck with both hands. Mathew's entire outer body seemed like it were made of tempered metal as David kicked him and almost broke his own toes.

"Who tried to kill me and Diana?" Mathew spoke.

"What are you talking about?" David replied in pain. He didn't know how to react thinking Mathew and Diana would have been dead even they were superhumans, and Valerie temporarily ignorant of their fate.

"You know who tried to kill me, and why. Tell me now or so help me, I will let Diana take you to hell." Mathew's cold and adamant eyes stared into David's eyes.

"It wasn't my fault. I couldn't do anything about it." David almost choked as he was now gasping for air.

A few screams could be heard outside and inside the property, but the three guild members ignored them. Kyle ensured they had their privacy and intercepted one of the security guards coming to protect David. Diana patted David and took away his cell phone. She tossed the phone to Valerie, and Mathew then tossed David backwards onto the sofa letting go of his neck. Mathew stood in front of David while Valerie and Diana were to one side.

"Who?" Mathew asked again.

"The Australian government. There's this Dr. White who's in charge of this special military unit. He had the satellite equipment moved. They knew you would try to get it, so once you left US territory they tracked you. They threaten to kill me if I didn't help them. I tried to get them off my back by giving you the empire." David explained.

"Is that why you accepted the fifty million pounds as half payment for mine and Diana's death?" Mathew countered.

David's face showed less fear, but it was ever present in his voice and eyes. "It's not like that. That much money can help a lot of needy people. It's just business."

Lee and Cynthia were clearly inside the large house and moving towards them. "You will give us all the information you have on these people." Mathew commanded as he grabbed David by the arm and forcefully moved him to a work computer in the study next to the living room.

Lee and Cynthia entered the living room and watched Valerie and Diana standing near the open arch way of the study. "All clear." Lee said.

Diana nodded and focused her attention back toward Mathew and David. David unlocked the computer and brought up all he had on the Australian contacts and records. The information was not of any direct value as to who and what, but there were leads to what the android assassins were and what Australia might be up to. Mathew motioned Lee to copy the information on the computer. Lee walked up to the computer and touched it. His armor linked directly with the hardware and copied everything to include the server hard drives, and backups. He changed the passwords and unlocked the encryption software.

"Done." Lee said after copying four terabytes in less than two minutes.

"What are you going to do with me?" David asked looking into Lee's black helmet blast shield being he was closest to him and Mathew was behind Lee.

Lee stepped to the side, "Don't ask me, I'm not in charge."

Mathew walked out into the living room. "What was the plan after Mathew and Diana was found dead?" Valerie asked as she motioned him to come back into the living room.

"Did you really think I would not find out and come after you?" Valerie asked with an angry and inquisitive expression.

"The Australians have more of those machines, and they plan on using them." David said.

"What are they exactly?" Lee asked entering the living room.

"I don't really know. I know they are lethal and strong enough to kill superhumans."

"Why didn't you warn us, we could have helped you?" Valerie asked.

"You can't stop them. They are too strong."

"Always thinking like a businessman." Cynthia stated.

Diana walked up to David and touched his arm injecting him with poison created by her phasing particles. "Nothing personal, but we have all the information we need, and like you said, it's just good business." She coldly said as David fell to the ground paralyzed, his heart stopping a few seconds later, never to start again.

Cynthia was about to move towards Diana, but Kyle appeared next to her and grabbed her hand tightly. She turned towards him and relaxed, knowing that there was nothing she could do and what was done was for the benefit of the group, to include her.

"Diana?" Valerie said hoping to have gotten more information from David before his fate was decided on.

"What? Ask me why again later when one of those things comes to kill you." Diana said without any sign of guilt.

"Okay well take care of the body, we have to get back to Henry." Lee said almost without a care in the world.

They got rid of the body, and burned down the ranch. The entire group returned to the Malleson estate prior to 10 pm. Kyle and Cynthia mingled with the guests, while the rest of the group went to the library.

Henry was wondering what happened while they were gone, so he sat down in a chair waiting for them to report everything.

"Lee told me about everything you did, and as requested I did some checking on my own. Lee is whom we were really hoping to find, so your services are no longer needed. You have another job waiting for you." Valerie handed Henry a legal document giving Henry full custody of his two children.

Henry read the documents quickly. "I don't know what to say; how?" Henry said in disbelief.

"We had everything expedited. It is all legal, I had to get two judges, ten lawyers, and three police departments out of bed early, but it was worth it." Valerie said, and handed him another paper indicating his name with several bank accounts totally $40 million US dollars. The third packet of papers was federal revenue documents indicating the already full payment of $20 million in taxes for that year.

"Your new job will be to raise those two kids." Valerie smiled, as well as everyone else in the room.

"There is a limousine outside waiting to take you to our private jet. Your children are waiting on the plane for you; tell my assistant where you want to go for a thirty day vacation. In that time, make arrangements to where you want to permanently live.

My legal team will stay with you for the next six months to make sure you have everything you need. If you need them longer, just let me know." Valerie said.

"Consider that your early Christmas present." Lee said as he walked up to congratulate him.

Henry stood up, shook his hand and hugged him.

"If you ever need anything I am there for you." Henry told Lee, with teary eyes.

"Same here Wildman. Just don't be a stranger." Lee smiled. Everyone hugged Henry good luck and they left the library laughing and smiling. Henry said his farewells to every guest, Kyle, and Cynthia as all were waiting in the main banquet room to give him best wishes.

Lee, Diana, Mathew, and Valerie saw Henry off at the limo. It was bitterly cold, but no one seemed to care as they waved good bye. The night was young as the guests left shortly after midnight. The three couples were left alone in the mansion's dance floor enjoying the occasion. Valerie stopped the music and Mathew passed out wine glasses.

"I want to declare that Lee is now an honoree member of the Guild with no name." Valerie announced.

Cheers was said along with a toast. Valerie asked the one question they all wanted to know most. "Having said that. Lee what guild name shall we call you from now on?"

Lee looked at the team. "You can call me Alpha."

Mathew smiled and signed, "Alpha it shall be." Valerie translated.

They toasted once again and the music was turned back on. Valerie wanted to slow dance with her husband so each person paired up after she changed the music. Mathew and Valerie were in their own romantic little world, as were Kyle and Cynthia. By default, Lee was with Diana. Lee was happy to have Diana's body touching his, especially since she didn't seem to mind one bit. This was the first time he was really close to her and had time to talk without anyone or anything interrupting their moment.

"You never asked me why I agreed to stay with the team." Lee said.

"I figured you would tell me in time. But I'm curious why you don't have a problem with us killing people."

"Well, I'm not perfect and I don't like it, but I understand sometimes there is no way around it. I have seen coldblooded hearts, and you guys aren't coldblooded with the intent on killing whoever for pleasure or gain. My adopted father told me destiny was what you make it. I want to help people and fight crime, but I feel there is something else I'm supposed to do, so here I am." Lee answered.

"In today's society, what we did and still do is considered criminal, so I think you might be in the wrong place." Diana stated.

"No, Diana, I'm right where I want to be."

"Where exactly do you think you are?"

"The team needs my help to steal from the rich to give to the poor, but my main reason to stay with the team is to be with you."

"Really?" Diana almost blushed, knowing he was serious

about his intentions toward her.

Even with the high heels, Lee's eyes were evenly leveled with hers. Her breath was sweet and skin soft as silk. She smiled peacefully as Lee stared into her eyes, also smiling.

"What is it?" Diana stopped smiling, almost annoyed by his constant staring and smirk.

"Does this mean I can call you goddess now?"

Diana sternly stared deep into Lee's blue eyes. "You can call me Diana."

"As you wish Diana, goddess of the Hunt." Lee gently tighten his embrace around her waist, and passionately kissed her.

Diana returned the kiss with like passion, forgetting about the fate of everyone and everything as Australia moved towards mass political assassinations and world domination.

# Author Notes

This book was written with the intent of telling two separate stories during a timeline that in the end will merge. There is no dominating evil villain in the two stories, but there is an evil entity in the form of the Cardigan Foundation. The past two books built a framework of the world situation, governmental agencies, and introduced the character of Cindy Owens (known as Samantha Brooks and Mirage in the book, He is Known as Ego). This book addresses the character of Lee Frost, and the thief guild which he joins. I established the epic story to be told in eight books. Each book either starts a new storyline or continues the story from where it left off in previous books. There are five major storylines in the entire epic series, focusing on the Eternal Champions, the nameless guild, the Galactic Guardians, the five ghosts, and the final battle for Earth. There are two sub-stories dealing with Jean and Jared, and Estabon and Sharon.

I used places and times as best as possible to show the extent of the characters' extensive resources. It is also to establish a point in time for the reader to reference. The major timeline of this book is in late 2005 up to 2012 which is also the timeframe for the end of the second book, He is Known as Ego. The detailed descriptions in some scenes were specifically done to help the reader see the action and enjoy the moment. I could have been more descriptive with people, locations and settings, but I didn't want to distract the reader from the interaction of the characters or the situation. There are many characters in the book, but what might be most difficult to follow are the numerous names which many characters have or had. I included a list of characters and aliases to help in following the characters and who was who. I also tried not to over emphasize the fact that sign language is a major part of communication with several characters, so I rely on the reader to understand when sign language is being used and translated. It was easier to do this with the first two books because mental telepathy was used to communicate between characters, but the characters in this book don't have that ability and have to rely on sign language, even though they can speak.

There are also technical points which the reader might notice if they know about weapons for example, like the fact that I describe Lee's weapons as laser rifles or just plain rifles. A rifle by definition is a weapon that was given that name for the rifling features in the bore of the weapon. I didn't want the reader to think of the weapons when envisioned as a shot gun, minigun, or a futuristic blaster. I wanted the reader to imagine a futuristic rifle like the end of a 50 Cal sniper rifle or a 30mm cannon. I didn't use those descriptions because the term rifle is more common and allows for a wider range of a vision of what the weapons look like. If there is still any confusion as to what the weapons might look like, I would say they come closest to the weapons used in a Gundam anime. I used the same logic in other points making it easier for the reader to understand what is going on and picturing the story in their minds. Characters phasing through objects is described as the character spreading their molecules, but that is not the case for all the characters that can phase. I went into detail with Cindy's character on phasing and invisibility because her abilities are unique and can affect the normal plane of existence as opposed to Diana who cannot make things phase beyond an inch or so from her skin. Diana cannot see if her vision is blocked while she is phased, while Cindy can because she is in another plane of existence. I hope the details or lack of details on the science or physics of things does not or didn't overwhelm the reader's enjoyment for the story.

In the preface is a very small snap shot of the history which led to the setting of this book, but it also reveals a snap shot of the superhero epic series. The powers and abilities of the characters in this book are diverse, but not strongly balanced like the superheroes in The Eternal Champions group. There are limitations, and superhumans can and do die; however, what readers should remember is that the story is based on the heroes that primarily live until the end of the story. The main characters in this book are Lee, Cindy, Mathew, and his team. Not that I don't like to kill off a character, but that the story has already been created to encompass them to a future which is told at the end of the book series. I could technically kill off a character and bring him or her back to life with the use of Joshua, but that would not follow the integrity of the characters or storyline which I have already created in my mind and on paper. I attempted to show the moments of weakness and strengths of the characters. I tried to bring out life experiences or expertise which they lived through or know by their actions and things they hint to. An example would be Lee's knowledge of military black operations which he was trained on as a child and in his own traveling with law enforcement agencies while undercover. Cindy's ease in spying and using her powers not having to experiment or find things out by trial and error are already inherit in the story of the book since she was already accustomed to moving around and changing the molecular structure of things she touched in a history of three years of spying on the mafia bosses and thieves.

The book ends with the heroes wining to a certain degree, but there is still much to be done, and villains in the world are bent on bringing in a new and dark future, which will be more evident in the future books. Unfortunately, the storyline for this book continues in books six, seven, and eight of the series. But don't despair, because the answers to the alien connection with Earth and what war is brewing are in books four and five. I hope you enjoyed this book and look for the upcoming sequels.

| | | |
|---|---|---|
| The Galaxy Is Ours | - | book 4 |
| Masterminds | - | book 5 |
| Superhumans From the Past | - | book 6 |
| Ultimate Assassins | - | book 7 |
| Last Hope for Earth | - | book 8 |